"You still suspect my motives, don't you?"

"You think," Brett continued, "I indulged your aunt hoping that she'd alter her will."

"Yes," Eve agreed. "The way you're indulging my sister hoping she'll persuade me to give way. Leave her alone, Brett! She doesn't have any experience of men like you."

"And you do?"

She had a glimpse of his grimly purposeful expression as he yanked her toward him, then his mouth clamped down hard on hers, his arms like steel about her rib cage. Her skin tingled, and her lips moved under his, opening to let him in. Only when he moved to mold her against him did she begin to struggle for sanity and sense. With both hands she pushed him away from her.

"Talk about hidden fires!" Brett's soft tone was infinitely disturbing. "I've been concentrating on the wrong sister."

Books by Kay Thorpe

HARLEQUIN PRESENTS

HARLEQUIN ROMANCES

KAY THORPE

the inheritance

Harlequin Books

TORONTO • NEW YORK • LONDON
AMSTERDAM • PARIS • SYDNEY • HAMBURG
STOCKHOLM • ATHENS • TOKYO • MILAN

Harlequin Presents first edition July 1984
ISBN 0-373-10710-2

Original hardcover edition published in 1984
by Mills & Boon Limited

CHAPTER ONE

'A MILLION dollars!' Fleur repeated, reading the magic words a second time to make certain there was no mistake. 'It's like something out of a dream! I knew today was going to be special—I just knew it!'

Watching her younger sister's pretty and expressive face across the breakfast table, Eve Brockley damped down her own inner excitement, aware that it stemmed from a different source. 'It's only an offer,' she pointed out. 'We don't actually have the money as such. It could take months to settle the legal side. This one letter took ten days getting here.'

'But we know it's coming eventually. That's all that matters.' Velvety brown eyes sparkling, Fleur tossed the letter back across the table. 'The first thing I'm going to do tomorrow is go and buy that dress I wanted from Carmella's. I can't wait to tell the crowd—they're all going to be green!'

Then don't tell them, Eve wanted to say, but knew it would be a waste of breath. Nothing would persuade Fleur to keep a thing like this to herself. To be fair, there was no valid reason why she should. The legacy was real enough. As Laura Cranley's only living kin they inherited her whole estate between them without controversy, control of each half contingent only upon the legatee in question having reached the age of twenty-one years. At twenty-four, Eve was well qualified, but Fleur was in by only two months. Lucky Fleur!

5

She would have hated to be bound by any trustee ruling.

It was still hard to take in. They had never even known Aunt Laura except as a vague figure in old photographs and a signature on a card at Christmas. Their own mother had only been a small girl when her elder sister had gone out to Florida to marry her American rancher, and contact between them had been at best spasmodic. Their mother's death two years ago might have brought about a meeting, except that Laura herself had been ill at the time and unable to travel. Some man named Hanson, describing himself as a friend and neighbour, had sent formal condolences in her name. Since then there had been nothing—until this.

Eve picked up the legal missive and read it through again slowly. One thousand acres—that was a lot of land. A going concern too, if this buyer was willing to pay such a price for it. It was hardly likely that Aunt Laura had run the place alone in the six years since she had lost her husband, so who would she have turned to for help? A good foreman, perhaps? In those tales of the Old West the ranch foreman had always been the mainstay of the whole outfit. She had to smile at herself there. She was even thinking in Western-style clichés!

'I think we should take a look at what we're inheriting before anything else,' she said, without giving herself any further time to consider the pros and cons. 'How would you feel about a trip to Florida?'

Her sister's piquant features lost their dreamy expression, long blonde hair swinging as she turned from her contemplation of the pale March sunshine through the kitchen window. 'You must have read my mind,' she laughed. 'I was just visualising myself lying on a long white beach surrounded by all these super-looking men! Not that any of them would know I was an heiress, of course. I'd hate to be wanted just for my money!'

Eve smiled back. 'As if any man would want you just for your money! You're the prettiest girl in Midhope. Everyone says so.'

'It's hardly that big a town,' Fleur responded, but she sounded well pleased by the compliment. She studied Eve for a moment, eyes taking on a new expression. 'Are you serious? About Florida, I mean?'

'Why not?' Eve tried to keep her tone practical. 'It would help speed things up. Anyway, wouldn't *you* like to see the ranch too?'

'Kind of savour the feeling of owning all that land before we sell it?' Fleur nodded slowly. 'Yes, I suppose I would.' Enthusiasm was creeping in as she spoke. 'We could even finish up taking a holiday on the Gulf after everything was finalised. I always wanted to visit New Orleans!' Her face clouded a little. 'But what about our jobs? I don't have any holiday entitlement until the end of April.'

'We're hardly going to need jobs,' Eve pointed out. 'Not the kind we have now, at any rate. We both have valid passports, and I shouldn't imagine we'd have any trouble with visas. Considering the circumstances, I doubt if either your boss or mine would insist on a full month's notice. We could be on our way in a couple of weeks.'

Fleur was looking at her as if she had never really seen her before. 'We only received the letter about half an hour ago,' she said, 'yet you sound as you've had plans made for months! Did you already know about it?'

Eve shook her head, her shoulders lifting in a faint shrug. 'It's just that I've been wondering for some time whether to have a complete change, that's all. Only I wasn't sure what—or where. This letter is like the answer to a prayer. Not just from the money angle, but because it offers a chance to try something totally different.'

'For a limited period.'

Hazel eyes flickered. 'All right, for a limited period. But it's a stepping stone, isn't it? Instead of beginning a new way of life right here in Midhope we do it from a spot that's at least halfway to where we want to be.'

It was Fleur's turn to shake her head. 'I'm not all that sure I know what you're on about, but if it means not having to listen to that infernal dictation machine any more I'm all for it! Thank heaven it's Saturday—I could'nt bear going in to work with all this on my mind!'

Neither, thought Eve, could she. There was going to be a lot to do, and little enough time in which to do it. Fleur was not the only one surprised by the speed of decision. Only last night she had lain awake for hours looking into a future devoid of highlights. Marrying Terry would have been no answer. If she really loved him enough there would have been no doubts in her mind to start with. America was half a world away. Out there was the adventure and excitement her heart secretly craved. No more waiting for five o'clock and escape from the deadly day-to-day sameness of office routine. She would be free to indulge her own inclinations—to roam the range from morning till night if she so preferred.

Romantic! she chided herself humorously. Modern-day ranch life probably had little in common with that depicted in a thousand Western films. Horses would mostly have been replaced by jeeps or Land Rovers, the cattle themselves transported the whole distance to their ultimate fate by rail. Yet a thousand acres was still a lot of land to look at. Worth seeing, even if only for a time. The sooner they got there the longer they would have. That was the only reason she was in such a hurry. For all her adult life she had played safe, thinking about that rainy day her mother had always set such store by. Now it was time to break out.

'What about money?' asked Fleur suddenly, breaking in on her thoughts. 'The fares will cost a packet, I imagine. Do you think this Mr Shane might offer an advance?'

'We don't have to ask,' Eve responded. 'I have enough in the bank.'

'For both of us?' Fleur made a ruefully smiling little gesture. 'I don't have a bean. Well—not a lot, at any rate.'

'It's all right, I can cope. We only need tickets one way, after all.'

'Meaning we'll have more than enough to come home on!' Fleur laughed out loud. 'Oh, it's going to be wonderful! Just imagine never having to worry about money again!'

Just imagine never having to worry about anything again, thought Eve dryly. The past two years had been anything but easy. Fleur was a darling and she loved her dearly, but there was no escaping the fact that she had little sense of responsibility when it came down to mundane matters like paying her share of the bills. 'I'll give it you later' was her usual promise, too frequently forgotten. Eve couldn't find it in her heart to blame her too much. She herself had a reasonably well paid job as secretary to the sales manager of the firm for which they both worked, while Fleur still battled it out in the typing pool. She was far more interested in clothes and fashion than Eve had ever found time to be, and was always threatening to go and try her luck in London where, she appeared to believe, her looks alone would qualify her for overnight success. With visions of the kind of situation in which those self-same looks allied to such blithe naïveté could land her, Eve considered any extra financial sacrifices she made a small enough price to pay for peace of mind.

'I shouldn't tell anyone about all this until I've had chance to confirm things,' she said now with some return of caution. 'I have that day in lieu of Monday. I could telephone this Mr Shane.'

'You mean keep it all to myself the whole weekend?' Fleur laughed and shook her head. 'I couldn't! Don't start being a pessimist now. How could there possibly be any mistake?' She finished her coffee in a single gulp and got up from the table. 'Anyway, I have to dash. Paul Strickley is picking me up at ten. He's just bought another car—second-hand, of course,' she added with a touch of newly acquired condescension. 'I think I might go for a Porsche myself.'

And there went one person who was going to have little trouble adjusting her ideas to her income, reflected Eve with ironic amusement as her sister disappeared in the direction of the bedroom they shared. The Mini outside was the only car either of them had ever driven on a regular basis. From that to a Porsche was a step her own mind as yet refused to take.

The table needed clearing, but she made no immediate move to do it, studying the letter for a third time as if half expecting to read something fresh between the lines. After a moment or two she put it down again and rose to her feet, crossing the small though pleasantly furnished living room to open a drawer in the dark wood dresser and take out the tin box Fleur called 'memory lane' in reference to its contents. In here were photographs and mementoes dating back to the day when the Brockley family was whole and complete. Normally Eve would have lingered over the snap of her father taken only weeks before his accidental death when Fleur was three years old; today she passed it by in her search for another, older photograph she remembered seeing.

The one she did eventually turn up was brown with age and curled at the corners, but the man and woman shown were distinguishable enough, the latter dwarfed by the sheer height and breadth of shoulder of her husband. Laura had not been unattractive in her own right, yet she too must have suffered from comparison with the little sister destined to become such a beauty—although the greater age gap might have made all the difference. As a child, Eve had grown accustomed to hearing people comment on Fleur's picture-book blonde curls and angelic features; had learned to accept that her own short mid-brown hair and ordinary face were never likely to excite the same interest. While in latter years she had come to realise that feature for feature she and Fleur shared very much the same inheritance, she had also recognised the futility of attempting to emphasise the likeness with a change of hair colour and style, settling instead for a simple,

uncluttered line which made the most of its
smooth, glossy thickness and dark gold highlights.

I won't let you down, Aunt Laura, she thought
now, gazing at the faded snapshot. Not without a
struggle, at any rate. If you'd wanted us to have
the money instead of the ranch you'd have said
so—wouldn't you?

There was no real answer to that question, only
this feeling deep down. A new life beckoned, just
the way it had beckoned Laura all those years ago.
It had at least to be tried.

The flight was delayed. Darkness had already
descended by the time they landed in Miami. In
accordance with instructions received, they went
straight to the airport hotel and checked in for the
night, too weary from the long journey to want to
do anything much beyond eating a light meal and
falling into bed.

Morning brought a revival of both spirits and
energy along with the breakfast ordered through
room service.

'It's exactly like it is on the films!' exclaimed
Fleur, gazing out through the double-glazed
window at the curve of Freeway visible from this
angle. 'Just look at the heat shimmering off all
those cars! It must be in the eighties.' She
stretched luxuriously. 'Not that you'd know it,
with the air-conditioning in here. This is the
life!'

'Don't get too attached,' Eve warned lightly.
'We still have to get to Ockeechobee county.'

'Don't I just love that name!' Fleur turned from
the window, coffee cup in hand. 'What time did
Mr Shane say we'd be met?'

'Ten o'clock in the lobby. That gives us just over

an hour to get ourselves together. It's going to be a long drive at a top speed of fifty-five.'

'If whoever is doing the driving sticks to the letter of the law, and I'll bet not many do.' Fleur sounded unconcerned. 'What are you going to wear?'

'Something comfortable,' Eve answered. 'Slacks and shirt, probably.'

'Then I'll do the same. The new blue set should be just the thing.'

Eve had been thinking more in terms of something *old* and comfortable. She hid a smile. Little of what Fleur possessed in the way of clothing came under that category. Her travelling choice yesterday of pale pink boiler suit and floating scarf had drawn many admiring eyes, impractical though it might have appeared at first glance. Eve herself had concentrated on a wardrobe she believed she would find useful on a ranch. She was here to learn, not to sit around.

The last fortnight had been hectic, to say the least. There had been so much to do, so many details to take care of. Saying goodbye to old friends had been the most difficult part. Terry was the only one to whom she had admitted her plans, and his response had not been encouraging. Leaving aside his own feelings, she didn't have the right to deprive Fleur of her opportunity, he had said. Eve had not agreed. She still didn't agree— not wholly. If after a suitable period of time Fleur was as desperate to sell out as she seemed to be right now then they could reconsider, but for the moment they owed Aunt Laura the compliment of attempting to live in the home she had provided. If the lawyer had been at all disconcerted by her announcement of intent when she had phoned him, he had concealed it well. All expenses had been met by the estate, the first-class air tickets delivered by special courier from Midhope's largest travel agency. Wonderful what money could do, as Fleur had remarked. Certainly they had not received the same standard of service with regard to their Spanish package deal the previous year.

They were down in the lobby by ten minutes to the hour. Assured by reception that all charges had been taken care of, they found seats in the area and watched the comings and going about them.

One man in particular drew Eve's eyes as he came in through the main doors and moved across to reception. He was well over six feet in height, shoulders wide and hips lean in the tailored grey shirt and pants. A wide-brimmed hat was pushed casually to the back of the dark head, revealing a face hewn from solid granite. Some instinct set her heart beating faster as he spoke briefly to the male receptionist, then he was turning his head in their direction, blue eyes penetrating even from this distance.

'Lordy, lordy!' murmured Fleur at her side when he started towards them. 'Is *he* something!'

Too much, was the thought that flashed through Eve's mind. Too big, too male and too almighty sure of himself! It was there in the very way he moved, his casual dress, his total disregard for the glances turned his way. Animosity leapt in her, crackling like something alive. She had never been one for snap judgments, yet she was doing it now, and for no adequate reason as yet.

'Brockley?' he asked. His voice was deep, with just a hint of a Southern drawl. 'I'm Brett Hanson from the Diamond Bar. Are you ready to travel?'

'We shall be when we know a little more about who we'll apparently be travelling with,' said Eve calmly before Fleur could speak. 'Why don't you sit down, Mr Hanson? Take the weight off your feet, as they say. I'll order coffee.'

The blue eyes studied her for a long, calculating moment, dropping to assess every curve of her body in a manner which made her squirm inwardly before returning to her face. His smile was slow and faintly sardonic. '*I'll* order coffee, if that's what you want,' he said. 'Take your time, by all means.'

His gesture brought a nearby bellboy on the run. He gave the order succinctly, ignoring any possible job demarcation lines. Orders, Eve gathered, could always be relayed to the appropriate department. No doubt that was the way he ran all things.

'Are you the one who sent condolences in Aunt Laura's name when Mom died?' asked Fleur as he took a seat at her side.

'My father,' he acknowledged easily. 'Same initial. He's Bart. Short for Bartholomew—which he wouldn't thank me for telling you.' The eyes resting on the vivacious little face turned up to him held a light of indulgence Eve for one was swift to recognise. 'We're neighbours. The Diamond Bar borders the Circle Three. You could say it surrounds it, apart from the east rim. The story goes back a long way. There were several spreads originally along our stretch of the Kissimmee River. My family bought out all but the Circle Three over the years. Jos always refused to sell while he was alive.'

'So apparently did Aunt Laura.' Eve met the glance he turned her way without flinching. 'So you waited till she was dead. That offer Mr Shane mentioned did come from the Diamond Bar, didn't it?'

'Sure.' There was the faintest of lines between the black brows. 'I'd say it was a fair price.'

'It isn't the price I'm talking about,' she said. 'Just your way of going about things. You could at least have waited till she was cold in the grave, so to speak, before trampling all over it!'

The blue eyes had hardened. When he spoke it was with a cutting edge. 'Get your facts straight before you start sounding off. Laura agreed to grant me buying rights in her will more than a year ago, only she never got round to changing the original draft.'

'Can you prove that?'

A muscle tautened suddenly in the strong jawline. 'My word's usually good enough.'

'I'm sure it still is.' Fleur was looking at her sister with startled incomprehension. 'Eve, what's got into you?'

Eve wasn't all that sure herself. She hadn't meant to say all she had. The words had come on their own. Having gone this far, however, she was not about to start backing down. 'I'm simply trying to do as Mr Hanson suggests and get my facts straight,' she said.

'The name's Brett,' he responded on the same hard note. 'We don't stand on ceremony in this part of the world. If you're trying to tell me you've had a better offer, why not come straight out and say it?'

'But we haven't!' Fleur was sitting forward in her seat, her gaze flitting anxiously from one to the other of them. 'There was never any question of not accepting your offer. Tell him, Eve!'

'Supposing we leave it where it is for the present,' he suggested dryly in face of the pause. 'Including the coffee. I'd as soon get off the ground before lunch.'

'Off the ground?' repeated Fleur. 'You mean we're flying the rest of the way too?'

The smile was for Fleur and Fleur only. 'Quickest way of getting there. I've a Cessna waiting ready refuelled—or it should be by now. We're less than an hour's flying time away.' He looked back at Eve, the warmth vanishing. 'How about it?'

She shrugged, refusing to give way. 'Why not?'

Brett Hanson rose along with the two of them, taking a slim wallet from his breast pocket and extracting a couple of notes which he tossed carelessly on to the table. Eve wondered fleetingly what would be thought should someone else appropriate the money before the waiter arrived with the coffee, but decided it was hardly her concern. She felt in an odd mood altogether, her nerves as tense as bowstrings. Never in her life before had she treated anyone the way she had treated this man, yet she couldn't bring herself to regret it. He set her on edge with every word, every flicker of an eyebrow, every arrogant inclination of his dark head. It was like having an invisible line drawn between them—one across which she had no intention of stepping.

They took one of the airport runabouts out to the private sector, finding the green and white Cessna waiting for them in front of the hangar. Brett loaded their luggage himself, going through the pre-flight checks under Fleur's rapt attention. Seated behind the two of them, Eve had only to look at her sister's face to realise how devastatingly far and fast she had fallen. Fleur had always been impressionable, but never more so than now in a new country with a type of man so totally outside her experience. He was outside hers too, Eve acknowledged, only she wasn't going to let that faze her. He wanted something they owned; that had to give them the whip hand.

Fleur kept up an endless flow of conversation once they were in the air. Eve gave up listening, concentrating instead on the unfolding landscape below. Lake Okeechobee came and went, giving way to the south central flatlands dotted with trees and waterholes and the occasional homestead. It was difficult to associate so much emptiness with their initial impressions of the Floridian scene.

They followed the river for the last few miles, coming in low over the cluster of buildings which constituted the Diamond Bar headquarters. The neat row of mobile homes set down some quarter of a mile or so from the main house were for the use of the ranch hands, Brett informed them. Most of them were married, some of them with children who went to school in the nearest town by bus each day. Only the single men still slept in the traditional bunkhouse.

The landing strip was some distance away beyond a stand of trees. Brett put them down gently, taxiing to a halt in front of the small hangar. An open jeep stood waiting by the side of it, and he transferred both passengers along with their luggage before putting the plane away.

The full heat of the midday sun beat down mercilessly on the crown of Eve's head. She knew now why Brett elected to wear a hat. Once on it was apparently forgotten, because he had made no attempt to remove it even in the air. Perhaps he slept in it too, she thought with irony.

'Is it always as hot as this?' asked Fleur as their host came back to slide behind the wheel.

'It's still spring,' he said. 'Best time of the year. Gets humid later on, although the rains cool it down some. Most folk make for the coast weekends.'

'You mean the owners?' queried Eve coolly. 'Somebody has to look after the property.'

'On a rota basis, maybe.' He started the engine and slammed into first gear without glancing in her direction. 'Hold on. It isn't a smooth ride.'

He wasn't joking. There was no road as such, just a rutted track formed by the passage of wheeled vehicles. Squeezed into the rear seat along with some of the overflow of luggage, Eve hung on grimly, trusting that they would be changing cars for the rest of their journey out to the Circle Three. If the Hansons could afford to pay a thousand dollars an acre for land, they could surely afford to have some decent roads laid on what they already had!

Seen from ground level, the collection of buildings forming the Diamond Bar homestead were many and varied. One had a petrol pump outside, with a couple of pick-ups standing in line for refills. Both drivers wore typical cowboy outfits of denims, boots and wide-brimmed hats, yet there wasn't a horse in sight. They lifted casual hands in greeting as the jeep passed, a gesture as casually returned by Brett.

The ranch-house itself was low and rambling, fronted by a wide porch over which bougainvillea climbed in colourful profusion. The sweep of grass separating it from the main yard area had been recently mown and watered, leaving every blade shimmering with moisture in the brilliant sunlight.

'Welcome to the Diamond Bar,' said Brett as he swung himself from behind the wheel. 'I'll get Maria to show you your rooms if you want to wash up before we eat.'

'Are you saying the Circle Three is too far away to reach today?' asked Eve, trying to retain some sense of proportion. 'We weren't anticipating putting you to this amount of trouble.'

'No trouble,' he assured her, lifting suitcases from the vehicle to stack them on the porch step. We've plenty of room.'

'That wasn't the question.'

He turned to look at her then, his expression stony. 'I could get you there inside half an hour, but I'm not going to.'

Eve looked back at him steadily. 'I assume you have a good reason?'

'An excellent one,' he agreed. 'Until Alex Shane gets down from Orlando to finalise matters you don't have any business on the place. The law requires proof of identity.'

'I have all the necessary documents with me,' she said. 'Surely . . .'

'It isn't up to me.' There was finality in the tone of his voice. 'Alec said Friday, Friday it's going to be!'

Today was Tuesday. The thought of being under any obligation at all to this man was bad enough, to spend three whole days under the same roof would be more, Eve thought, than she could bear.

'The house *is* still standing, I suppose?' she asked without bothering to hide her scepticism. 'After all, a lot does seem to have been taken for granted where Aunt Laura's intentions are concerned!'

Brett ignored Fleur's shocked protestation. His attention was wholly on Eve, his mouth set like a steel trap. 'Laura spent the last few months of her life right here at the Diamond Bar,' he said on a clipped note. 'I'd say that gives me a better idea of what her intentions might have been than a niece who never even met her!'

'But you never actually brought her round to changing her will,' Eve flashed. 'That has to mean something.'

His breath came suddenly hard and heavy. 'It means,' he said through his teeth, 'that I'm coming pretty close to losing my rag with you! I'm not sure what it is you're after, and I don't aim to find out on the doorstep.' He paused there, visibly controlling the surge of anger. 'I'll straighten you out later,' he promised, and it was no trick of inflection that made it sound like a threat.

An elderly woman of probable Cuban descent came out from the house at that moment. She was wearing a dark dress which looked far too heavy for the climate, yet her dark skin was quite free of the perspiration Eve could already feel dewing her temples. Brett turned to her abruptly.

'See our guests in, will you, Maria. I'll bring the bags.'

Eve hesitated before moving after the woman. It was only Fleur's whispered plea that finally put her feet into motion. The entrance hall was part of the huge living area, sectioned off by the arrangement of furniture. Cool greens, spicy lemons and lots of sparkling white created an excellent background for burnished wood and leather, the shaded windows softening the light to a pleasant glow. Of Bart Hanson himself there was no sign.

Maria led the way across the room to an inner hallway, and down a corridor lined with several doors. Their rooms were next to each other, and spacious, the beds king-size, the adjoining bathrooms beautifully fitted out. Lunch would be served in fifteen minutes, Maria told them expressionlessly. They were the only words she had spoken. Whether she was always as taciturn, or reserved the attitude for unwelcome visitors, was a question Eve determined to ignore. They weren't going to be here long enough for it to matter.

'Why are you being so horrible to Brett?' demanded Fleur the moment they were alone. 'It isn't like you, Eve!'

'I don't trust him,' Eve acknowledged, and wondered fleetingly if that was the whole truth. 'He had everything cut and dried before he even saw us.'

'But it is cut and dried, isn't it?' Fleur sounded confused. 'Mr Shane said we were unlikely to get a better offer.'

'But that's just it. It *was* only an offer. We never officially accepted it.'

'Surely that's splitting hairs!'

'I don't see why. I object to having my mind made up for me.' Eve had moved over to the open window, looking out through the fly-screen at the pastoral landscape beyond the homestead boundaries. 'Aunt Laura must have had good reasons for not changing her will—especially when she was living right here under this roof for several months before she died. I want to know what they were.'

'You could try mental confusion for starters,' advised the sardonic voice from the doorway.

Brett dropped his burden of suitcases to the floor and straightened, his size in harmony with the room. His eyes had a dangerous spark. 'Let's try holding back on the assumptions for a spell, shall we? There'll be time to talk.'

'Brett, I'm sorry.' Fleur obviously saw no reason why she should be involved in the coming confrontation. She didn't even glance in her sister's direction, her eyes fixed anxiously on the tall Floridian. 'I don't know why Eve is doing this. I thought it was all agreed that we took your offer.'

The blue eyes softened visibly as he looked at her. 'Don't worry about it. We'll work something out. Tell me which suitcases are whose and I'll split them up.'

Many of the male friends left back home would have given a great deal to be on the receiving end of that smile, reflected Eve wryly. She couldn't blame Fleur for feeling the way she did, but neither could she relinquish the role she had elected to take. If she had to battle alone against this man and his aims, then she would do it. For Aunt Laura's sake she would take on the world if necessary!

CHAPTER TWO

THERE was no time to change before the meal. Eve contented herself with a swift handwash and a comb through her tousled hair, coming out from the bathroom to find Fleur waiting for her, the latter's expression a cross between mutiny and apology.

'I suppose you're thinking I should have backed you up!' she burst out before Eve could speak. 'Well, I can't. Not when I don't even know why you're being this way!'

Eve said gently. 'You don't have to back me up. You don't have to be any part of it.'

'I can't help being a part of it, can I? The ranch is half mine—or it will be when everything is finalised.' Fleur drew herself up with visible resolve. 'I want you to drop it, Eve. I've as much right to a say in the matter as you have!'

'Of course you have,' Eve agreed. 'But surely any ultimate decision should be made after we see the ranch, not before? It was Aunt Laura's home for a number of years. Don't you have any feeling about that at all?'

'Not the way you obviously have.' Fleur bit her lip, gazing at her sister with resentful eyes. 'You had it all planned before we left home, didn't you? You knew you'd no intention of accepting that offer, yet you let me go on believing we were going to share a million dollars!'

'It isn't so much a case of not accepting it as of waiting to see exactly what it is we're selling,' Eve explained patiently.

24

'You mean it could be worth more?'

'Perhaps.' It wasn't what she had meant at all, but it would do for the present. 'As you just said, we're not even in possession yet. At least let's wait till we are.'

The pause was lengthy, the agreement made with some reluctance still. 'All right. Just promise me you'll stop treating Brett like some crook, that's all.'

Eve studied the pretty face for a moment, seeing the faint flush creeping under her skin. 'Do you really like him all that much?' she asked softly.

The blonde head lifted, eyes shining with a new light. 'He's the most *fabulous* man I ever met. And he likes me, too, I can tell. Don't spoil things for me, Eve!'

Eve looked at her helplessly, not at all sure how to react. They had known Brett Hanson for little more than a couple of hours all told. How was she supposed to react? 'He's at least ten years older than you,' she pointed out, without much hope of getting through. 'He may even be married.'

'He isn't. I asked him just now when we were taking my cases through. Oh, not right out. I said would his wife be here for lunch too.'

Very subtle, thought Eve wryly, refraining from comment. Fleur was too accustomed to having the opposite sex at her feet to consider taking any great pains with the art of subterfuge. Being the kind of man he so obviously was, Brett Hanson would be only too well aware of the effect he was having—and would almost certainly have the experience to nip it in the bud, if he wanted to. And if he didn't want to? The emotion that thought elicited was difficult to analyse. Protectiveness, she told herself on an oddly defensive note; she only had Fleur's welfare at heart.

'We'd better go,' she said. 'We wouldn't want to be late.'

The two men were together in the living room. The wheelchair in which Bart Hanson sat came as a shock they had only bare moments to assimilate. Why Brett had failed to warn them, Eve had no idea. Right now it hardly mattered. The onus was on the two of them to strike the right note.

It was easy to see the relationship. The father was simply an older and more weathered version of his son. On closer approach, one could also perceive that not all the lines were those caused by age. This man had suffered pain, perhaps was suffering it still, although there was no sign of it in the eyes lifted appraisingly.

'It doesn't take any birth certificate to tell me you're Laura Cranley's kin,' he said bluntly to Eve as his son performed the necessary introductions. 'You look much the way she did when she first came out here all those years ago—apart from the pants. Women didn't wear the pants in any sense in those days!'

'Times change,' she smiled, taking his measure with what she hoped was a certain accuracy. 'These days they're for comfort, not effect.'

His mouth stretched briefly. 'Just as peppy with the answers too!' The expression underwent a change as he turned his attention to Fleur. 'Aren't *you* the pretty one! That hair real?'

'He's teasing you,' interposed Brett before Fleur could find an answer. 'Cut it out, Dad. She only just got here!'

'And more than welcome to stay.' Bart put

large, fleshless hands to the wheel rims of the chair. 'Isn't it time we ate?'

'Lead the way,' his son invited.

The dining room was on the west side of the house. Like the rest of the Hanson home, it was spacious. Four places had been set at one end of the long, gleaming table. Brett saw both girls seated one on each side of his father at the head before taking his own place next to Fleur—to the latter's unconcealed pleasure. The blue eyes meeting Eve's across the width of the table challenged her to question the arrangement.

Shorn of the hat, his hair sprang thick and vital. Everything about the man was vital, Eve acknowledged with that same inner reluctance. In any gathering he would automatically command attention, and not just for his physique.

Maria served the substantial meal without speaking a solitary word. 'She never was much of a talker,' acknowledged Bart in answer to Eve's casual comment after the woman had brought in coffee and departed. 'Husband's the same. Brett's mother hired the two of them more than twenty years ago. They've run the place between them since she went. My second wife wasn't interested in domesticity.' He registered the swift flicker of expression in her eyes with a faint smile. 'You'll hear the story soon enough, so you might as well have it from the horse's mouth. Four years ago I married a woman twenty years my junior. She left me a couple of weeks after this happened,' indicating the chair he still occupied. Briefly his eyes sought those of his son, the irony increasing. 'No fool like an old fool!'

'How did it happen?' asked Eve on a level note without looking in Brett's direction.

'My horse had a heart attack and collapsed while I was in the saddle,' came the equally level reply. 'We both rolled down the same bank, only he landed on top of me.'

'I'm sorry.' It sounded inadequate, but it was the only comment possible.

His shrug was philosophical. 'After nearly three years I've made the adjustment. Lucky I had a son to take over from me. I planned on an early retirement anyway when he was thirty. I just anticipated by a year, that's all.' He paused, his tone altering. 'Brett tells me you're planning on staying with the Circle Three?'

'Only for a little while,' put in Fleur quickly. 'Eve thinks Aunt Laura would have liked us to live in the house for a few weeks.'

'Could be. She had real feeling for the place. It's going to need some airing out, though. Shouldn't imagine anybody's been in since the dust-covers went on—unlesss Connors has been keeping an eye?' The last with a glance in his son's direction.

'It wasn't his concern.' The tone was short.

'Supposing my aunt had recovered from this illness of hers, whatever it was, and wanted to go back home?' suggested Eve mildly.

The answer came in flat, unemotional tones. 'She had a brain tumour. She knew she was dying long before her mind started going.'

Shock and dismay robbed her of any ready response. She could only sit there gazing at him with darkened eyes until Bart himself took pity on her.

'She wanted to be with people she knew—that's why she came here instead of a nursing home. We brought in a resident nurse the last couple of months. She didn't suffer any more than could be helped—drugs took care of that. She died peacefully in her sleep.'

'Poor Aunt Laura,' said Fleur with sympathy. 'If only we'd known!'

'You couldn't have done anything,' Brett assured her, and received a melting glance.

'You're just trying to make me feel better about it.'

'All the same, he's right. You couldn't have done anything for her,' said Bart. 'No use dwelling on it. Coming back to the house, we'll get somebody over there to see to things as soon as Alex Shane gives the go-ahead. Might take a couple of days, but there's no rush anyway. Only too pleased to have you here.'

Eve smiled, making certain mental reservations. 'We're very grateful for the hospitality, Mr Hanson, but we wouldn't want to abuse it.'

'You won't do that. A couple of pretty faces to look at brightens up any man's day!'

She didn't need to see the satirical quirk of a dark eyebrow to sense Brett's reaction to that statement. His father had been right the first time: Fleur was the pretty one. She met the blue eyes expressionlessly. Let him mock. He would get no rise out of her. She knew exactly where she stood when it came to looks.

'How far is the nearest town?' she asked on a casual note.

'We're roughly midway between Sebring and Yeehaw Junction,' Brett answered. 'Depends what you'd call a town. There's Leesville five miles west. General store, saloon, diner—not much else.'

'Big enough to have its own deputy sheriff and jailhouse,' put in his father mildly. 'It's a real pretty little place. If you've nothing on this afternoon, why don't you drive the girls over to take a look?'

'Another time, perhaps,' Eve started to say, but Fleur was ahead of her.

'Oh, that would be lovely! Would you, Brett?'

'Why not?' He sounded easy enough about it. His glance found Eve's again, the glint meant to be seen. 'You might like to keep Dad company if you're not interested.'

'No way!' exclaimed the latter. 'She didn't come all this way to sit with an old man!'

'No, I didn't,' agreed Eve blandly, 'but I'll sit with you.'

His smile was appreciative. 'In that case, I'll let you.'

Fleur was looking like a cat offered a whole bowl of cream. Having Brett to herself was a bonus she had not anticipated. 'I must change first,' she said. 'You don't mind waiting, do you?'

'Not when it's likely to be worth waiting for,' he responded lightly, and was rewarded with her most scintillating smile. 'I'll see you out front when you're ready.'

They all four adjourned from the dining room at the same time, with Eve only just managing to repress her instinct to start clearing the used dishes; the Hansons' reactions aside, Maria herself would probably not appreciate any interference with her routine. They were living in a different world. She had to accustom herself to the change in status.

'Come on out on the porch,' suggested Bart as Fleur disappeared upstairs to effect the promised transformation. 'This time of year it's too good to sit about indoors.'

Brett made to move to help him as he wheeled

the chair in the direction of the outer doors, pausing in his own progress to pick up the hat he had worn previously from a pale leather sofa, although he forbore from putting it on. Eve had wondered initially why the wheelchair was not electrified. Watching the way Bart handled it, seeing the development of his shoulders and arms, she came to the conclusion that he might find some consolation in keeping at least one half of his body in good shape. The dark blue slacks he wore could not fully conceal the wasted muscles of his legs.

There were comfortable chairs and a low round table set out at one end of the wide porch. From here one could look out across the whole homestead to the gentle landscape beyond. There were comings and goings between the different buildings, but nothing like the hustle and bustle of activity Eve had half anticipated.

'Most of the hands are out on the round-up,' said Bart, sensing her unspoken question. 'It's a busy time of year.'

Her eyes switched from the scene ahead to the man leaning indolently against the rail close by. 'You don't ride with the men?' she asked on a light note not mean to deceive.

'Normally,' he responded without revealing any particular reaction. 'I had another job to do today.'

'You mean picking the two of us up?' with a faint lift of her brows. 'You could have delegated—we wouldn't have felt slighted in the least. I hate to think you've been torn away from more essential matters just for our sake.'

The irony had not escaped him; that was apparent from the fleeting expression in the blue eyes. He didn't move, but his stance seemed to harden. 'No hassle,' he said. 'The job will get done whether I'm there or not.'

'We've a good team,' agreed his father. 'Most of them have been with us for years. They'll be through before the end of the week, so if you're interested in seeing what goes on you'll need to make it in the next couple of days. Can you ride?'

'A little.' Eve had been on horseback exactly three times in her life, but she was not about to admit it. 'I suppose it would depend on how far I had to ride.'

'We're down on the south pasture,' said Brett. 'Half an hour by jeep to the gate. We only use horses to work the herd these days.' His tone was dry. 'You could see all you'd probably want to see from a safe seat.'

'I'd want to see everything,' she retorted promptly, holding his gaze. 'There isn't much point otherwise.'

He shrugged. 'I'll take you out there with me tomorrow, if you're that eager.' He shifted his glance as Fleur stepped from the house, a soft, deliberate whistle escaping his lips. 'Now that's what I call a sight for sore eyes!'

And wholly conscious of it, thought Eve in some wry amusement as her sister posed for a moment before moving towards their little group. She was wearing a multi-hued tube of a dress which clung to her slender shape, her feet clad in sandals that were no more than wisps of leather. As an outfit in which to visit what had sounded like little more than a one-street town, it was in a class on its own. Not that such minor concerns would worry Fleur; she was intent only upon the initial impact.

'I'm ready,' she announced brightly. 'I hope I didn't keep you waiting too long!'

'Hardly any time at all,' Brett denied, straightening away from the rail. 'You look good enough to eat!' He took up his hat from the table where he had dropped it and put it on, the twist of his lips barely defined. 'Just stay right here. I'll bring the transport over.'

There was a brief silence as he dropped down the step and moved off round the corner of the house. Bart was the first to break it.

'Watch you don't trip over anything in those heels,' he advised. 'Could be dangerous.'

A polite way of saying how totally unsuited to the occasion they were, acknowledged Eve ruefully, too well aware that Fleur would ignore the message even if she perceived it. Perhaps if it came from Brett she might listen, only would he bother? He saw Fleur as a pretty little thing to be indulged, but no more than that, she was certain. He wouldn't care what kind of foolish impression she might create in the minds of those who didn't know her.

The promised transport proved to be one of the long and luxurious wood-panelled estate wagons only seen this side of the Atlantic. Fleur's face expressed her delight as she took her seat beside Brett. Man and car both were so obviously all she could ask. Eve could only hope that this first flush of enthusiasm would fade as it usually did, yet she knew the circumstances were different. Brett had knocked her sister sideways, to put it mildly. If he realised it, and she was almost sure that he did, then it was up to him not to encourage her in any way. Surely he would see the sense in that?

'It's difficult to see you two as sisters,' commented Bart bluntly as the car drove off. 'You're as different as chalk from cheese!'

'She was always the pretty one,' Eve acknowledged, and heard the derisive snort.

'That's not what I'm talking about, and well you know it! That girl doesn't have a thought in her head worth a dime!'

Her answer was instant and unconsidered, every protective instinct in her springing to Fleur's defence. 'Perhaps you've found being in that chair gives you the right to say what you think without fear of contradiction, Mr Hanson, but I don't subscribe to that kind of indulgence. There's nothing sub-standard about my sister's intelligence!'

In the following pause Eve could feel herself start to grow warm with embarrassment. This man was her host; what she had said to him was unforgivable. She couldn't look at him. 'I'm sorry . . .' she began, but he held up a staying hand.

'Don't be. You're the first person I've met, apart from my own son, who doesn't see this chair as a reason for humouring me. I'm grateful for it.' The smile was faint. 'Not that it alters my opinion any, only let's get it right. I'm not criticising her brain power, just the use she makes of it.'

'You've only known her a couple of hours,' Eve protested.

'Long enough to make a comparison between the two of you. I'd be willing to bet you're the one who's kept things going financially since your mother died.' The smile came again at her lack of response. 'Not prepared to make a complete liar of yourself?'

'I made a lot more than she did.' The defences were still operative. 'It was only fair I should contribute the most.'

'But not all.'

'Fleur paid her share.' Eve shut out the mental rider to that statement. Sometimes was better than never.

Bart was looking at her with thoughtfully narrowed gaze. 'You're using the past tense. Does that mean you're decided not to go back to the same place at all?'

'We both gave up our jobs,' she admitted on an offhand note. 'There was no point in keeping them, even if we'd been able to get extended leave.'

'So what plans *do* you have for the future?'

Eve shrugged uncomfortably, not yet ready to discuss that question. 'We haven't decided. We're still getting used to the idea of owning all that land.'

'The land's no use to you unless you're capable of using it.' The pause was meaningful. 'Or are you considering learning?'

Eve looked back at him for a long assessing moment, her smile wry. 'Am I so easy to read?'

It was Bart's turn to shrug. 'From what Brett was saying before lunch, you haven't been going to any great pains to hide what you think about the offer he made.'

'*He* made? You mean you aren't involved?'

'I turned control of the Diamond Bar over to my son the day they told me I wouldn't be doing any walking again,' he said without emotion. 'I told you that at lunch.'

'I didn't realise you meant total control.'

'No sense in anything else. It's in capable hands.'

She bit her lip. 'I don't doubt it.'

'But you still don't trust his word when it comes down to what Laura intended?' He shook his head as she attempted to speak. 'That's between the two of you. I'm a biased witness. I warn you, though, he's set on having his way.'

'So am I,' she said flatly.

The pause stretched. When he did speak again she already had a very good idea of what he was going to say. 'How does your sister feel about it?'

'She wants to sell.' It was a waste of time prevaricating on that point when a simple question to Fleur herself would be all that was needed to clarify matters.

'She has an equal right.'

'I know.' Eve met his gaze honestly. 'Perhaps I'm being both selfish and stupid in wanting to hang on to something I know absolutely nothing about, but I'd at least like to see the place before we start making any decisions.'

'I guess it never occurred to Brett you'd be more than passing interested.' The tone was mild. 'So be honest with him. Tell him how you feel. Maybe you can come to some kind of compromise.'

'Such as?'

'Well, I daresay he'd be willing enough for you to stay on in the house.'

'As tenants?' Eve shook her head. 'Nothing personal, Mr Hanson, but I don't think that would work out.'

'Stubborn little cuss, aren't you?' He studied her for a long moment, his eyes shrewd. 'I don't believe that "nothing personal" bit. What did that son of mine say or do to antagonise you? I've known him get across people before, but never with the female sex.'

Eve could imagine. No doubt he only had to crook a lean brown finger to have all the women in these parts falling over themselves to please him. Fleur was a case in point. She lifted her shoulders.

'Just one of those things, I suppose. It's not one-sided.'

'So I gathered,' Bart said dryly. 'So sort it out between the pair of you. I've said all I'm going to say.'

Eve accepted the termination of subject without rancour, grateful for the tolerance already shown. That she could not expect the same forbearance where Brett Hanson was concerned she was already too well aware. That battle was still to come.

It was gone six before the other two returned. Eve was in her room changing for dinner, which was served early out here at seven. Fleur came in without bothering to knock, face lit by an inner glow.

'Did you wonder where we'd got to?' she asked ingenuously. 'Brett took me for a long drive after we left Leesville. He wanted to show me a bit of the Diamond Bar.' She laughed. 'It was only a bit too! He said it would take all day to tour the whole ranch—a hundred and eighty thousand acres. It certainly puts Aunt Laura's place in the shade!'

'You went there too?' Eve queried, conscious of the swift shaft of resentment.

'Only along the boundary fence. It's easy to see why Brett is so keen to join the land to his. It cuts right into the middle. A thousand pounds an acre, that's what it amounts to.'

'It's the going rate,' Eve responded evenly. 'I made a point of finding that out before we left. He isn't doing us any favours, Fleur. We could get that price anywhere.'

'Except that nobody else would want to buy it because of where it's situated.'

The words tripped too fluently from Fleur's tongue to be anything but a verbatim quote. The afternoon's excursion had served its intended purpose. Brett had Fleur wholly on his side. Eve tried a change of tactic, recognising its limitations even as she did so. 'Have you realised that once we accept the offer we'll have no further reason to stay in this part of the country?'

'Not necessarily.' The brown eyes held a determined light. 'Brett says we can stay on at the Circle Three as long as we like. It isn't the house he's interested in.'

'Generous of him.' Eve reached for the slim-fitting white cotton dress she had laid ready across the bed, pulling it over her head and down the length of her body in one smooth motion. Moving across to the dressing table, she sat down on the stool and took up her hairbrush, her every gesture forced. 'Dinner's at seven,' she said to the mirrored reflection of the girl behind her. 'Shouldn't you be thinking about getting ready?'

'You're jealous, aren't you?' said Fleur suddenly. 'You wouldn't be like this if Brett was attracted to you instead of me!'

'I couldn't care two hoots about Brett Hanson,' Eve denied, the words sounding hollow even to her own ears. She made herself go on. 'What I do care about is that you don't get hurt. He's not like the boys back home, Fleur.'

'You don't have to tell me that.' Both tone and smile were reminiscent. 'Brett's a man, not a boy. I never knew anyone like him before. He's so . . . so *sure* of himself!' And totally uncaring of others, thought Eve with anger, watching the expressive face. No doubt he found Fleur's swift infatuation both flattering and amusing; certainly he was making no effort to pull her back down to earth.

'You've only just met him,' she said without much hope. 'Don't get carried away.'

'You *are* jealous!' Fleur's mouth had taken on the familiar wilful line. 'Just leave me alone, Eve. I'm twenty-one, not sixteen! Brett recognises that much even if you don't!'

Brett needed straightening out in more ways than one, reflected Eve grimly as her sister flounced out of the room. And the sooner the better for all concerned.

CHAPTER THREE

IT was a long and lazy evening. Bart had looked out some old photographs taken at a ranch barbecue which both the Cranleys had attended. One of Bart himself laughing heartily with the two of them amply demonstrated the lack of animosity between the neighbours. It brought a hard lump to Eve's throat to see him standing on two good legs. No matter how well adjusted he claimed to be, there was no way he could not feel bitter inside at the memory of all he had lost.

'Sorry I don't have any more recent ones,' he said. 'You'll probably find plenty over at the house. Laura liked photographs—instant nostalgia, she used to call them.' His smile was reminiscent. 'She was a very likeable woman. Brett's mother thought the world of her.'

Eve would have liked to ask if he had any photographs of his first wife, but even though Brett appeared to be taking little interest, his very presence in the room put her off. Seated beside Fleur on one of the long, deep sofas, he was listening to what she was saying with a lazy half smile on his lips, one arm lying with apparent carelessness along the backrest behind her head where her nape had to keep brushing it. Catching his eye, Eve made no attempt to disguise her contempt. He was playing her sister along for one reason and one reason only—to get her on his side. It wouldn't matter to him that she might become emotionally involved.

'If you're still interested in coming with me tomorrow I'll be leaving at six,' he said casually over the coffee Maria brought through around ten. 'Think you'll make it?'

'Coming where?' asked Fleur before Eve could reply.

'The south pasture,' he told her. 'Your sister wants to see some action.'

'I'd like that too,' she claimed. 'I hope I'm included!'

'If you want to be.' There was no telling what he was thinking. His glance still rested on Eve's face. 'Well?'

'I'll be ready,' she said.

'We'll *both* be ready.' Fleur sounded just a trifle petulant.

'If you're all planning on being up before six an early night might not be a bad idea,' suggested Bart, glancing at the nearest timepiece. 'I'm going, anyway, if nobody minds. Twelve hours in this chair and I start to ache even where I can't feel!' His grin robbed the words of any element of self-pity. 'You'll be off long before I get myself together. I'll see you when you get back.'

Brett made no move to accompany his father, leaving Eve to draw the conclusion that help was not needed. Or perhaps it was simply that Maria's husband, José, provided any that was necessary. There was a moment or two of silence after Bart had gone. Eve was the first to break it, pretending to smother a yawn.

'Your father's right, an early night isn't a bad idea,' she said. 'I think I'm still suffering from jet-lag.' She got to her feet, eyes seeking those of her sister. 'Coming?'

Fleur smiled and lifted her shoulders. 'I'm not in

the least bit tired. I thought I might go for a walk before bed. Just a short one, of course, though I can hardly get lost, can I?'

'You might walk into something you hadn't bargained for,' said Brett easily. 'Snakes can choose the darnedest places to lie up for the night. I could do with a breather myself.'

Which was exactly what Fleur had been angling for, Eve reflected, and not very cleverly. But then she hardly needed to be clever. Brett was giving every impression of a man only too willing to follow her lead. Perhaps she was wrong about him; perhaps he really did want to be with Fleur for her own sake. A lovely face and a winning manner turned many a male head.

Rejection of that idea was instant and emphatic. Not Brett Hanson; he was too much the man in command. His plans for Fleur might well include the treatment she was asking for, but there would be no future in it. If only Fleur herself could be made to see beyond the dream world she had begun so swiftly to create!

Eve had been in bed almost half an hour before the faint sound of movement from the room next door told her Fleur had finally retired for the night. The knowledge should have eased her mind, but it didn't. Lying there in the darkness of a strange room thousands of miles away from all that was familiar, she found sleep impossible. Nothing was working out the way she had planned. Perhaps it never would. Aunt Laura had probably felt just as out of place when she had first come here, but she'd had the man she loved to cling to and learn from. Would they have done better, after all, to have stayed home in England and let the lawyers take care of everything?

And spent the rest of her life wondering what might have been missed? came the rueful acknowledgement. No, the journey had been necessary, even if things didn't work out. Only she had to give it a chance, didn't she? They had only been in the country a matter of hours. How could defeatism have crept in already?

She got up after another half hour of tossing and turning, pulling on a cotton wrap and belting it tightly about her waist. Where she was going she had no clear idea. All she knew was the need to be unconfined by these same four walls.

The house was quiet, all lights extinguished. She found the outer doors unlocked, stepping out into the warm and scented night with a small sigh of relief. That was better. If she could sit out here on the porch for a while she might clear her head of its jumbled, milling thoughts. She went over to the rail, resting her hands on it as she looked out over the ranch yard. Light pierced the darkness from several sources, although she could see no sign of movement. A dog barked somewhere not too far away, the sound answered by the whinny of a horse.

'Having trouble sleeping?' asked Brett from a dark corner of the porch. 'First night in a strange bed it's often that way.'

Eve's fingers had gripped the smooth wood in involuntary spasm. Now they relaxed again, although the rest of her body remained tense. She forced herself to turn without haste, eyes seeking the shape of him sprawled comfortably in the low chair.

'I didn't realise there was anyone else still up.'

His shrug was more sensed than seen. 'I was just thinking about turning in when you appeared.'

'Then don't let me keep you.'

'Why not? Now's as good a time as any to talk things out.'

Her heart thudded painfully once and was steady again. 'There's nothing to discuss—not the way you mean. I have my way of looking at things, you have yours.'

'And never the twain shall meet.' The tone was sardonic. 'You're forgetting one small but important factor. Your sister doesn't agree with you.'

'Tell me something I don't know,' Eve retorted smartly. 'What are you saying—that I should give way because Fleur wants me to?'

'She has rights.'

'So do I. Hers are no more important.'

'At least she's practical,' he clipped back. 'She knows her own limitations!'

Eve smiled with slow deliberation into the darkness between them. 'I don't plan on running the ranch myself. I'll find someone to do it for me—for us, I mean. This Connors your father spoke about at lunch. Is he the foreman?'

There was a pause before the answer came. 'It's his job to act on orders, not run the whole show.'

'Then who's been doing it since my aunt was taken ill?'

'I have,' he said flatly.

That fetched her up, but not for long. 'It had to be to your advantage.'

'How?' he asked on the same unemotional note. 'It's the land I made the offer on. Just the land. I'm not interested in anything else.'

Eve gazed at him, her eyes already well enough adjusted to pick out the hard features. 'Then why bother? Why didn't you just let the rest go?'

'Because it kept Laura happy to know the Circle

Three was still in business. She gave Jos her word she'd keep it going through her lifetime.' He waited a moment, his mouth taking on a slant when she failed to make any comment. 'It doesn't make any difference to you, does it? You still suspect my motives. I indulged her in the hope that she'd alter her will, is that what you're thinking?'

'Something like that.' She would allow herself no wavering of intent. 'The way you're indulging my sister in the hope she'll persuade me to change my mind.'

'Is that what I'm doing?' He sounded almost amused. 'It hadn't occurred to you, I suppose, that your sister might have other attractions?'

'Well, of course she has. That's a bonus, isn't it?' She tried to keep her tone even. 'It wouldn't occur to you that she might be vulnerable? Or don't you care?'

His laugh came low and mocking. 'I guess having to compete with Fleur's looks must have been a real strain on your better nature, honey!'

Eve said tautly, 'You aren't answering the question.'

'I don't feel any need to answer it. She's of age.'

'She doesn't have any experience of men like you!'

'And you do?' The twist of his lips was a taunt in itself. 'Suppose you start by telling me just which category I come under?'

'Con-artist,' she retorted with a curl of her own lip. 'You'd use anyone or anything to get what you want!'

'You reckon?'

'I reckon.' She moved jerkily away from the rail. 'I don't see much point in continuing this conversation.'

'Neither do I.' Brett was on his feet in one smooth action, covering the few feet of space between them before she could retreat inside. She had a glimpse of his grimly purposeful expression as he yanked her towards him, then his mouth was clamped down hard on hers, his arms like steel bands about her rib cage.

Eve stopped struggling after the first few seconds and let herself go limp instead, determined he would get no satisfaction from her that way. Only her body refused to stay unresponsive, her nipples hardening of their own accord beneath their flimsy covering, her skin tingling as the kiss changed character, searching deeper and more insistently, reaching a central core of heat and spiralling it upwards to reach every part of her.

Helplessly, she found her lips moving under his, opening to let him in, her limbs adjusting to accommodate every hard angle of the superbly fit body. Only when his hands came down to take her hips and bring her up closer against him did she come alive to what it was she really wanted, eliciting a wave of self-revulsion so strong he felt physically sick.

With both hands flat on his chest she pushed him away from her, fighting for sanity and sense. What he thought of her didn't matter. It couldn't be allowed to matter. She had given way to a momentary weakness, that was all. There was no way he was going to use that against her.

'Maybe I've been concentrating on the wrong sister,' Brett said softly, blocking her escape. 'Talk about hidden fires! That icy English maiden act of yours had me completely fooled.'

Eve put everything she knew into controlling her

voice. 'Don't read too much into it. You took me by surprise, that's all.'

'I'd like to take you.' He was still speaking softly, but on a note she found infinitely disturbing. 'Right here and now I'd like nothing better. It's been a long time since any woman got to me as fast. How about it? Shall we settle our differences in bed?'

Her head jerked, heat running under her skin. She had asked for that, she supposed, and he was not the man to let her forget it.

'Just put it down to experience,' she said with contempt. 'I'm no one-night stand! Now will you please get out of my way!'

He didn't move, looking down at her with narrowed gaze. 'You know, I think there might be a whole lot more to you than meets the eye. You knew I was still out here, didn't you? You came out for a purpose.'

'That's not true.' She attempted to break to one side, desisting as he shifted position to stop her. 'What possible reason could I have?'

'I'm not sure. All I do know is you deliberately provoked me into going for you.' One hand came under her chin, lifting her face so he could see it more plainly. The blue eyes held an unnerving light. 'You started needling me the minute we met. Why?'

Eve met his gaze without flinching. 'I'd have thought that was obvious. You walked into that lobby as though you owned the place, and everyone in it!'

'Meaning you'd have been more receptive if I'd come in on my knees?'

'Don't bother trying to ridicule me,' she retorted. 'I didn't like you then and I don't like you now. What happened a moment ago doesn't have any bearing. It's called chemistry. Bring certain elements together and they automatically react.'

'And how!' The tone mocked. Without warning, Brett slid the retaining hand downwards, drawing a gasp from her as his fingers encircled her breast. 'With prolonged results too. I wonder how long it would take to bring you to fusion point?'

Eve steeled herself against the emotive, nerve-tingling touch, denying him the pleasure of seeing her discomfited. 'Longer than you'd care to spend,' she said, curling her upper lip. 'I'm not fighting you, if that's what you're after. You can get your kicks somewhere else!'

'With your sister, you mean?'

'No!' Teeth gritted, she fought to keep her mind from dwelling on the slow, subtle movement of those lean fingers through the thin material. 'Just leave Fleur alone, do you hear? Leave her *alone!*'

'Make me,' he invited on the same soft note. He put his lips to the point of her jaw below her ear, feathering them down to the corner of her mouth with tantalising slowness. 'Stop blocking me over the Circle Three. I've waited a long time for that land.'

It was growing more and more difficult to withstand the sensations rising in her, to damp down the furnace in the pit of her stomach. She ached with the need to give way, the urgent desire to touch him the way he was touching her—to slide her hands inside the material of his shirt and feel the vibrant warmth of his skin, the ridging of muscle, the crisp curl of body hair. The answer came in a voice she scarcely recognised. 'And you can go on waiting!'

'Okay, so we both know where we stand.' He took the hand away, his smile mocking her involuntary movement. 'I guess it mightn't have taken that much longer after all. Not that there won't be other times. You make an interesting comparison, you and Fleur. How come she managed to stay so naïve?'

'Probably because the only men she's ever known have treated her with the kind of respect you don't seem to realise exists!'

'Hogwash! I said naïve, not inexperienced.'

Eve drew in a breath. 'Are you trying to suggest . . .?'

'I'm not suggesting anything. She's old enough to live her own life without protection from you. What I am saying is she still thinks all she has to do is put out her hand and everything will fall into it.'

'So far it always has,' Eve said wryly.

'Then she's going to have a rude awakening one of these days.'

'From you?' Eve was retaining control with effort. 'Use her to get at me, then tell her the truth—is that what you have in mind? I suppose you could call it being cruel to be kind, if you wanted to justify yourself. Only I doubt you'd ever feel the need to do that. So far as you're concerned, the end justifies the means. You want that land and you'll do anything to get it, no matter how underhand!'

'I'd stop right there if I were you,' he advised on a dangerously soft note. 'There's more than one way to get yourself put down.'

Her shrug conveyed an indifference she was a long way from feeling. 'I've said all I have to say.'

'Good. Then we'd better call it a day.' Brett

moved back away from her, expression steely. 'Still feel like making that trip tomorrow?'

If she said no it would be as good as admitting she was afraid of him, Eve acknowledged, stifling the impulse before it could draw breath. 'Of course,' she said. 'I'll be down here at six on the dot. So will Fleur.'

'That I'll believe when I see it.' He indicated the door. 'After you.'

She went ahead of him through the living room to the inner hallway, turning left to his right without a word of farewell from either side. Only when she was safely in her room did she let out the pent-up breath, leaning against the door to stare blindly across at the rumpled bed and wish she had never left it.

The ache deep inside her wouldn't let up. After a moment she put up a slow hand to her breast, tracing the still tingling imprint where that other hand had held her. Nothing she had ever experienced before had prepared her for this kind of need. Her own fault, she thought numbly. She should have stayed where she belonged.

The travel alarm woke her at five-thirty after no more than a couple of hours of fitful sleep. Wearily, wishing desperately that she had never agreed to go in the first place, she showered and dressed in jeans and checked cotton shirt, pulling on a sweater over the latter because the morning air was likely to be cool. A pair of walking shoes had to take the place of boots. It was doubtful if they would be doing any riding anyway—at least she hoped not. Yesterday's bravado seemed downright stupid in retrospect. Why couldn't she have simply told the truth? It would have made little difference to Brett's attitude.

Memory alone sent a quiver running through her. She had to get last night into perspective before she saw him again. For a moment or two she had allowed her guard to drop, but that was all. There was no way he could be sure of her inner feelings. If the truth were known, she wasn't sure of them herself. Body and mind were totally at odds with each other. Chemistry, she had called it last night—sheer basic chemistry. It could hardly be more.

She found Fleur still fast asleep beneath the covers. It seemed a shame to waken her, but she wouldn't be grateful for that kind of solicitude. Eve put a hand lightly on her shoulder.

'Fleur, it's ten to six! If you're coming you're going to have to hurry!

The only answer was a muttered protest and a deeper burying of the tousled blonde head into the pillow. Eve tried again. 'Fleur!'

'All right!' The tone was peevish, resentful, the brown eyes still tightly closed. 'In a minute!'

Getting her out of bed at eight o'clock back home had never been easy, Eve acknowledged wryly. Why should now be any different? She made one more attempt. 'Brett won't wait.'

'I said I'm coming.' Fleur still didn't move. 'Tell him I'm just getting dressed. It won't take me long.'

Eve gave up. She had done her best; it was up to Fleur herself now. She would stir herself the moment it penetrated that Brett might not be over-delighted to be kept hanging around. Whether she would do so in time remained open to doubt.

She found Brett waiting on the porch, a jeep standing ready. He was dressed in faded denims and matching shirt, the latter open at the neck on the triangle of dark hair. The hat he had on today looked well worn, its colour dulled to an overall peat. Meeting the blue eyes, Eve felt the heat rise under her skin. He hadn't forgotten, and he wasn't going to let her forget either. The slow, appraising glance he dropped over her was designed to underline that fact.

'You're early,' he said. 'Where's Fleur?'

'She'll be here.' Eve moved on past him to stand at the top of the wide step, drawing in a deep breath of the fresh and sparkling air. There was a wonderful clarity to the early morning light, the sky pale and cloudless overhead, with a promise of heat to come from a sun already well clear of the horizon. Others were astir before them. She watched a couple of the hands drive the last of a small herd of cows into a barn before saying tentatively, 'I thought you were purely in the beef market.'

'The dairy produce is for home use only.' Brett had come to stand beside her. 'We've a lot of mouths to feed.' Without altering his tone, he added, 'She's got three minutes.'

'I'll go and see what's keeping her,' said Eve quickly, but he shook his head.

'You already called her, didn't you?'

'Yes, but . . .'

'No buts. We leave at six whether she's here or not.'

She wasn't, of course. If she was up at all she wouldn't be bothering to make haste. With the fingers of her watch steady on the hour, Eve felt obliged to make one final plea on her behalf. 'At least give me a minute to check. If she is still in bed it's her own fault.'

'It's her own fault anyway,' was the only reply.

He moved on down the step to get behind the wheel, looking back at her with sardonically raised brows. 'Having second thoughts yourself?'

She was, but admitting it was something else. She made herself shrug and go to join him in the vehicle, conscious of the too close proximity of his shoulder to her own, of the taut line of his thigh beneath the close-fitting denim as he trod the clutch to select first gear. Had Fleur been with them, she would no doubt have been riding in the back again, but at least she would have been safe from the treachory of her emotions.

'Relax,' he advised dryly, putting the vehicle into motion. 'I never bite while I'm driving. Enjoy the ride.'

In many ways she did enjoy it, finding the scenery pleasant if a little uninspiring. The road they followed was wider and harder packed than the one from the landing strip, but no less dusty, cutting through the occasional stand of pine and at times coming within sight and sound of the river. Stranded wire fencing stretched along both sides as far as the eye could see, the grass beyond lush and green. There were cattle to be seen grazing across the river to the east at one point, a mass of brown in close formation—all steers, Brett informed her, and already sold, although they would be left to fatten a while longer on the rich spring grass before being shipped to the packing plants. Eve suspected his motives in making it sound so clinical a process, but he wasn't going to put her off that way, she told herself firmly. There was little room for sentiment where meat production was concerned, she already knew that. People had to eat.

Beyond the south gate, the roadway dwindled to

a two-rut track through the grass. A few hundred yards in they came on a camp area set to the leeward side of a clump of trees. There were a couple of pick-ups and a truck parked close by, and a string of horses tethered down by a moss-bearded oak on the bank of a stream. A coffee pot sat squarely on the portable range set down at the side of the truck, filling the air with an aroma that made Eve suddenly aware of her empty stomach.

The man who appeared from behind the truck was small of stature and as leathery as an old boot. It was impossible to guess his age. He could have been anywhere between fifty and seventy.

'Didn't expect you out again,' he commented casually as Brett slid from behind the wheel. 'The boys'll be through today.' The rheumy old eyes flickered in Eve's direction as she got out the other side of the jeep, taking on a faint gleam of interest. 'Guess you must be one of the Brits?'

'Watch your mouth, old-timer,' drawled Brett on a note of amusement. 'They're a sensitive breed.'

With deliberation, Eve put out her hand. 'How do you do?'

'*Jeese!*' From the way he was gazing at it she might have been offering him a rattlesnake. Gingerly he extended his own fingers, barely touching her palm before dropping the hand back to his side with a bemused expression. 'First time I ever shook hands with a female!'

'First time this female ever shook hands with a real live cowboy,' came the satirical comment from his employer. 'Any food left? We didn't eat yet.'

'Sure, plenty. How about ham and eggs?'

'No beans?' asked Eve brightly. 'I thought cowboys always ate beans!'

'Lady, you want beans, I got beans,' came the unmoved reply. 'Help yourselves to coffee while I get the pan going.'

Brett took a couple of sparklingly clean mugs from the bench table and poured for them both, handing Eve hers with a jeer in the blue eyes. 'You won't get a rise out of Chuck Rafferty,' he said. 'He's hundred per cent proof.'

She lifted her shoulders, her smile unconcerned. 'Just a mild joke. You wouldn't object to that, would you?' She tasted the coffee, making an appreciative face. 'It's very good!'

'It would be,' he said. 'You're the ones who can't make coffee.'

'A matter of opinion.' She sniffed at the delicious smell of frying ham already beginning to permeate the air. 'I don't normally eat very much for breakfast, but I never felt as hungry as this before.'

'I'll warrant you've never been up as early either.' Brett hoisted a foot to the back of the truck, leaning an elbow on his raised knee. 'You've a good healthy colour in your cheeks this morning. Different from the way you looked yesterday at the airport.'

'I was tired yesterday,' she retorted. 'The time difference isn't made up overnight. And before you say it, Fleur would look good no matter what. She's the pretty one, remember?'

The blue eyes were steady, unexpectedly lacking in mockery. 'There's a strong resemblance.'

Eve shook her head impatiently. 'You don't have to humour me.'

'I don't *have* to do anything,' came the smooth rejoinder. 'Okay, so you're not as immediately eye-catching as your sister, but you're not exactly the plain Jane either.' The pause held deliberation. 'Of the two of you, I'd say you had the better figure. Depends on preferences, of course. Some men go for boyish hips and small breasts. I prefer something to get hold of.'

Her colour had deepened but she maintained her composure. 'You made that fairly obvious last night.'

His smile was slow. 'I made a lot of things obvious last night. Come and eat. You're going to need plenty of stamina to get through today.'

CHAPTER FOUR

EATEN in the open air, the ham and eggs tasted wonderful. Eve finished every morsel, along with a second mug of coffee.

'That has to be the best meal I ever had,' she said when Chuck came to take the used dishes from them for washing. 'I never ate as much in my life!'

'Wait till you taste his Irish stew,' said Brett, handing his own empty plate across to the little man. 'We'll ride in from here, Chuck. Saddle up the Appaloosa, will you? I'll take the Pinto.'

Eve kept her expression carefully under control. At this moment she had a choice; she could either own up to her lack of experience or she could bluff it out. The Western saddles were very different from their Eastern counterparts. With any luck she could cope. The fact that it was a Western saddle Bart Hanson had fallen from, she thrust to the back of her mind. The circumstances were hardly going to be the same. Not even Brett could expect her to gallop the darned animal over unfamiliar ground.

It took the two men only a few minutes to get the horses ready for the road. With no offer of help forthcoming, Eve somehow managed to mount her own, settling down deep behind the comforting curve of the horn.

'You need your leathers adjusting,' said Brett, coming over to do it for her. 'Stretch your legs. You're not riding in the Grand National!'

She obeyed the injunction, immediately feeling more secure. Whether he had guessed the truth or not was hard to detect. The faint smile on his lips could mean anything. She steeled herself to meet his glance levelly when he looked up at her. There was no way he was going to get through her guard again. No way at all!

She envied the ease with which he swung himself on to the Pinto's back, gathering the two loose reins in the one hand to turn the animal's head with a mere touch of leather against silky neck. Eve's own reins had been knotted together to form one line, whether for her benefit or that of some previous rider she wasn't certain. She held them in both hands, feeding them through her fingers the way she had been shown her very first time on horseback. No use trying to run before she could walk. Once she gained confidence she would try experimenting.

Contrary to expectations, she felt totally at home within minutes of moving out. The saddle helped, of course. There was so much more of it. The Appaloosa mare had a smooth gait, though she shook her head from time to time in protest at the unfamiliar pull on her mouth. Eve forced herself to loosen up, taking both reins in the one hand and resting the other daringly on her knee. A wave of sheer well-being ran through her. Nothing to it. She couldn't fall off if she tried!

Brett had moved up slightly ahead after they crossed the stream, following the trail through the fringe of trees to open country. The break into a slow canter was followed by her own mount without any urging from her, causing her a momentary panic before she adjusted to the motion. If Brett had done that on purpose to unnerve her he was going to be disappointed, she thought with some satisfaction. On a horse as comfortable as this one balance was no problem.

The bellowing of cattle was audible some minutes before they reached the herd, the haze of dust kicked up by milling hooves hanging like low cloud on the near horizon. Eve could feel it in her throat and eyes as they rode in, and envied Brett the hat he wore, which at least afforded some slight protection. Not that the dust seemed to bother him at all; he was probably too accustomed to it.

The noise and activity notwithstanding, the whole proceeding was obviously under tight control, each man allocated a certain job. Eve watched one rider rope a calf and pull it clear of the main body of animals to where another cowboy on foot was waiting to take it from him. The jab of a needle, the swift smoking pressure of an iron, and the bawling calf was back on its feet and high-tailing it out to join its agitated mother. The acrid stench of singed hair lingered in its wake.

'I'm going in to help!' shouted Brett, bringing the Pinto up close so she could hear him above the general din. 'You'll be okay for half an hour or so?'

'Fine,' she shouted back. 'Don't worry about me—I'm happy to watch.'

The last statement was some way from the truth, but she had asked to come. Had she given it any real thought at all she would have imagined that branding was done by other means in this day and age—an indelible dye, perhaps. The red-hot irons looked cruel, even though the animals themselves seemed to suffer no after-effects. The Circle Three brand would no doubt be applied in exactly the same way, she reflected. Tradition died hard. The men out there working the herd were using the same methods their grandfathers would have used before them, proud of their skill with rope and mount. In fairness, it was difficult to imagine any other way of doing it. Certainly no wheeled machine could do what these horses could do, no matter how skilful the driver.

Brett had changed mounts, riding into the herd on a rangy grey. In seconds he had a calf roped and clear, recoiling the lariat the moment the noose was lifted and heading right back into the fray. Man and horses were as one, all senses united. Even from here Eve could see the flexing of the long thigh muscles as Bret signalled changes of direction, a sight which brought a curl of sensation down deep. Last night she had felt that same lordly demand—and been as quick to respond. Too quick, but she hadn't been able to help herself. Why was it that women were supposed to be so different from men when it came down to purely physical arousal? What she had known last night was nothing more.

What she had known last night was still here in her too. Watching him now, she wanted his touch, his attention, the closeness of the hard lean body. She had roused him once; she knew she could do it again. Whether she would grasp the opportunity should it be presented was something else. No one-night stand, she had said, but it went deeper than that. No casual affair could ever give her the kind of fulfilment she sought.

With the Appaloosa seemingly content to stay on the spot as long as required, she allowed herself to relax, leaning her weight back into the cantle.

She was going to be stiff by the time the day was out; already she could feel her muscles starting to protest against the unaccustomed usage. If Brett didn't come back for her inside the next ten minutes or so she would take a slow walk round the perimeter of the camp just to keep herself limber.

How long he planned on staying here she had no idea. From a spectator's point of view, the novelty was shortlived. One day she would perhaps be capable of taking part herself, although a lot of things had to fall into place before then. So far the dream remained a dream, and if Fleur had her way it would never be anything else. Was she being so unreasonable in wanting something more than money? she wondered. Couldn't Fleur see that happiness couldn't be bought? In the Circle Three they would have a home—a real home. The flat had never been more than a place to sleep and eat.

If her mother had still been alive she would have been in accord, Eve was certain. In fact, if she *was* still alive she would in all probability be the legatee, and the present problem would never have arisen. A sigh escaped her. Wishing wouldn't bring her back, so why waste time in doing it? Life had to be lived looking to the future, not the past.

Paradoxically, she found herself wondering what all their old friends were doing at this precise moment. It had only been a couple of days, yet it seemed years since they had left Midhope. The sudden memory of Terry's face when she had told him her plans brought a shaft of pain—conscience, she acknowledged ruefully. She hadn't loved him, and she had known it, yet she had let him go on believing in her. He would get over it, she comforted herself. At twenty-six he had all the time in the world to find someone who would care for him the way he deserved to be cared for. If it came to that, so did she—only maybe she deserved it less. Trying to play fair by everyone was no easy task.

It took a moment for the yell to penetrate her consciousness. Startled, still uncomprehending, she looked at the cow bolting towards her, then made a frantic grab for the horn as the Appaloosa wheeled unbidden to head the animal off. How she stayed in the saddle during those following seconds she never knew. Certainly there was no question of which of the two of them was in charge; the mare was intent only on her job. Hair flying, body unmercifully jolted, Eve hung on like grim death until one of the mounted cowpokes came thundering up, grinning all over his face, to turn the cow back in the right direction.

Brett arrived out of nowhere, reining in beside the now quiescent mare as Eve pulled herself together. He was grinning too.

'Teach you to let your mind wander!' he said. 'That's a cow horse you're riding.'

'There's nothing like being put wise after the event,' she retorted with sarcasm. 'It's a pity I didn't fall off, then you could have had a real laugh!'

His shrug made light of her anger. 'You didn't fall off, so what's the beef? If you'd any doubts about handling the animal you had time to say so back there before we set off.'

Eve looked away, biting her lip. He knew. He had known all along! She could have killed herself for all he cared!

'You weren't in any danger until this happened,' he said, reading her mind with unnerving accuracy. Okay, I should have warned you. If I'd thought about it I would have. Guess I'm just not used to having amateurs about the place.'

'How long does this go on?' she demanded stiffly, indicating the whole frenetic scene with a jerk of her head.

'As long as it takes.' His tone had hardened. 'If you're bored it's too bad. You wanted to come.'

He was away again before she could find an answer to that, heading for the action. Eve watched him go with fury bubbling up inside her. Did he really believe she was just going to sit here waiting until he deigned to take pity on her? If so he could think again!

The mare responded to her urging without hesitation, breaking straight into a canter as she dug in her heels. She was riding without thinking about it now, body settling to the rhythm. Brett could play cowboys as long as he liked; she was going home!

Her rage had dissipated a little by the time she reached the gate, but there was still enough left to keep her going. Chuck came to take the Appaloosa's head as she slipped to the ground, surprise and curiosity written plain on his lined face.

'Brett not coming?' he asked.

'Not yet,' she said. 'He'll be along later when they're finished. I'm taking the jeep.'

'Sure.' He was already unbuckling the girths, more concerned with animal than human.

The key was in the ignition where Brett had left it. Eve started the engine and selected what she hoped was reverse gear, ignoring the harsh grating sound as she fought the lever through the stops. She had never even attempted to drive a vehicle like this one before, but in this mood she was ready for anything. If Brett wanted transport there was plenty more to choose from.

With plenty of room to manoeuvre, she found little difficulty in backing up for the turn, lifting a hand in response to Chuck's wave before changing into first and heading for the track. All she had to do was follow the fence wires down to the main intersection, then turn left. It wasn't even nine o'clock. There was every chance Fleur might still be in bed when she reached the house.

What she was going to say when she got there she hadn't even considered yet; there would be time enough to think about that on the way. For the present she was concerned only with putting distance between herself and that man back there. The thought of his reaction when he found her gone was satisfying. With any luck, he would think she had wandered off in the vicinity, and waste some of his oh, so valuable time looking for her. It might be hours before the truth occurred to him, and by then it would be too late. The knowledge that she was going to have to face him again some time she pushed to the back of her mind. He would be furious, no doubt, but so what? There was little he could actually do.

She had gone some distance before the elation began to give way to a faint sense of shame. What did she really expect to gain from this? she asked herself. What could she hope to gain? Brett wasn't stranded; he wouldn't even be inconvenienced to any degree. And supposing he had been? Did her behaviour benefit an adult person?

At length she brought the jeep to a halt, sitting there gazing disconsolately through the windscreen while she tried to work out what she was going to do. Going back was one answer, yet pride still held the upper hand. Even if she did return, Brett wasn't going to let it pass. He would think nothing of ridiculing her in front of the other men. No, she had made her decision and she had to stick by it, right or wrong.

It was only when she reached the intersection of roads that the idea crystallised in her mind. If she carried straight on she would be travelling north— the same direction in which the Circle Three lay. Lawyer or no lawyer, there could be no harm in just taking a look, could there?

The thought was all it took. Unlike the rutted track she had just left, the new route was smooth and hard-packed, making driving a great deal more pleasurable. The Diamond Bar homestead lay some-where over to her left beyond the tree line. If Fleur was up and around she would not be in the sunniest of moods—one more reason, Eve told herself, for not going back any sooner than she had to.

One thing she was going to have to buy herself was a hat of some kind, she reflected, feeling the heat beating down on her unprotected crown. No matter how thick, hair was no substitute. The broad brims worn by the men were not just for effect. They served a dual purpose in both shading the vulnerable area at the nape of the neck and keeping the sun out of the eyes, dependent on which way they were tilted. Having come this far, she might just as well make a real day of it and carry on from the Circle Three into Leesville to find something suitable for feminine wear. She had thirty dollars tucked into the back pocket of her jeans. That should be enough.

A loop of the river cut across her path some distance on. Once across the wooden bridge, she saw the huddle of buildings ahead and to her right. The narrow road she reached a moment later had an entrance arch made from unstripped logs, with a sign below it bearing the interlooped rings of the Circle Three brand. Eve stopped the jeep and sat there looking at it for several moments, thrilling to the feeling of ownership. Brett was not going to take this away from her, not without a fight. No one was.

The general layout of the ranch yard was much the same as at the Diamond Bar, though on a very much smaller scale. Eve brought the jeep to a halt in a cloud of dust, switching off the engine as a man wearing the inevitable denims appeared at the open doors of the nearest barn-like structure.

'I'm looking for a Mr Connors,' she said clearly. 'I believe he's the foreman here?'

Without taking his eyes from her, the cowhand raised his voice in a stentorian shout. 'Lady for you, Wade!'

From another building some twenty or thirty feet away appeared another man carrying a halter in his hand. He was tall and lean, his hair bleached by the sun to a shade which enhanced his already remarkable good looks. No more than the late twenties, he was the total antithesis of the vague picture Eve had formed in her mind.

'Hi!' he said easily. 'You looking for me?'

'Yes,' she acknowledged. Having got this far she wasn't at all sure what she had had in mind. 'I'm Eve Brockley.'

His expression underwent a swift and subtle alteration. Dropping the halter by the door of the barn, he advanced to hold out a hand, his smile white. 'We heard you'd arrived—glad to see you. Brett let you find your own way here?'

'He's down at the south pasture,' she said evasively. 'I thought I'd take the opportunity to have a quick look round, that's all. I realise I'm not entitled to enter the house before it's officially signed over.'

'Wouldn't know about that,' he responded. 'That lawyer guy locked the place up after he and Brett finished going through it, and took the keys away with him. Guess there's nobody entitled to go in there till he says so.'

'Were they looking for anything in particular?' asked Eve on a casual note.

'Couldn't say about that either. They sure took long enough.' He paused, a curious expression in the pale blue eyes. 'There's two of you, isn't there? You and your sister?'

'Fleur, yes.' The hesitation was brief. 'I didn't set out to come here—it was a spur-of-the-moment idea.'

He nodded. 'Well, seeing as how you are here maybe you'd like to take a look around?'

'Yes, I would,' she agreed. She got out of the jeep, letting him close the door again for her. Something about him prompted confidence. 'I still find it difficult to believe I'm really here at last. I only wish we'd managed to make it while Aunt Laura was still alive. You must have known her well?'

'She was a fine woman,' he said. 'I owe her a lot.'

She glanced at him sideways. 'Including your job?'

'Sure.' He wasn't in the least put out. 'She judged by ability, not age. Not that there weren't those who thought they knew better.'

'Was Brett Hanson one of them?'

It was his turn to slant a glance, a certain caution in his eyes. 'He's been running the place over my head since Laura got too sick to bother about things. If he's taking over the Circle Three I'll be out of a job anyhow.'

'If you're asking me if we're going to sell out, the answer is not if I can help it,' said Eve levelly. 'Only I warn you, I'm fighting my sister as well as Brett.'

'Well, you've got one ally.' His expression had lightened. 'Laura wouldn't have wanted to see the Circle Three come under Diamond Bar brand.'

'Are you sure about that?'

'Sure I'm sure. Why else would she have kept on refusing to sell?'

They had reached the barn. Standing at Wade's side looking into the dim reaches, Eve said softly, 'I've been given to understand that she promised to grant buying rights to the Diamond Bar on her death. Does that sound likely?'

There was some slight hesitation before he answered. 'If she did it must have been because she was being pressured.'

Eve sighed. 'It's a pity she didn't put in some clause to the effect that we had to live here and work the ranch to inherit at all. That would have settled the whole question.'

'Maybe she had some inkling you'd feel the way you do,' he said. 'You're a lot like her.'

'So I've been told.' She made a decisive movement. 'Time will tell.'

The tour of the immediate area took up a couple of hours. So far as Eve could see, everything was in tip-top order. Their own round-up had been finished more than a week, Wade told her, the cows and new calves turned back to grass. The actual selling of marketable stock was usually handled by the owner, he said. As Brett Hanson was running the place in her stead, then it was up to him to find a buyer. So far nobody had turned up to view the herd as a prospect.

Brett probably hadn't even bothered to look for a buyer, Eve reflected angrily. He wanted the land, he had said, nothing else. With the stock unsold there would be no new influx of cash to keep the ranch solvent, hence a greater pressure on her and Fleur to get out. So she would find a buyer herself, if needs be, the moment she had the authority. Wade would know how to go about it. With Wade Connors around they would have all the help they needed in running the Circle Three. Just a year, that was all she asked. One short year!

Apart from ascertaining that it was a single-storey dwelling with a long front porch like the one at the Diamond Bar, she didn't go near the house itself. Peering in windows seemed somehow wrong; there would be plenty of time for exploration later when they had the keys.

'We'll be moving in at the weekend,' she told Wade before taking her leave. 'Any cleaning that needs doing we can tackle ourselves.'

'One of the wives would be glad to give you a hand,' he told her. 'You've only to say.' He put out a hand, his grin appealing. 'I'll be looking forward to Saturday—boss!'

Eve drove away feeling a great deal more confident about everything. Once she got Fleur away from the Diamond Bar and Brett's influence it would be easier to convince her. She *had* to convince her!

Leesville proved to be just as pretty a place as Bart had predicted, its main street fringed with palms and colourful flower beds. The little restaurant had red leather seats and formica tables, though the seafood platter Eve chose from the menu was beautifully presented. The sound alone of Key-Lime pie was a temptation. Her appetite, however, was not equal to the challenge, so she made do with a coffee instead.

'You're from England, aren't you?' said the young blonde waitress presenting the check. 'Gee, I've always wanted to do Europe! Are you here on vacation?'

Eve smiled. 'I'm rather hoping to stay. Do you know the Circle Three at all?'

'Sure.' There was an odd change of expression. 'We heard about the ranch being left to a couple of English girls, only everybody thought the Diamond Bar would be taking it over. Isn't that right?'

'No.' Eve used the flat negative with deliberation, aware that the word would spread like wildfire. The sooner people stopped taking things for granted round here the better! 'I've just been to see Wade Connors,' she added. 'He seems more than capable of running a ranch.'

'Wade's capable of a whole lot of things.' The tone was brittle. The girl studied Eve for a moment with a certain obvious appraisal. 'He doesn't owe Brett Hanson any favours, that's for sure.'

'Hey, Sue-Anne!' came the bellow from the man at work behind the counter. 'You taken root over there, or what?'

'On my way,' shouted the girl. She grimaced at Eve. 'Got to go. Have a nice day now!'

Eve would have given a lot to know what the girl had meant by that odd remark. Wade himself had said he would be out of a job if Brett took over the Circle Three, yet at the time she had thought little of it. She supposed it was really none of her business if the two men were enemies, providing it didn't affect the running of the ranch. If she and Fleur stayed, Wade would be the one they had to place all their trust in, but if he had been Aunt Laura's own choice then they could hardly go wrong.

The general store just a block away from the restaurant sold just about every item imaginable. There was a whole rack of hats in various colours and sizes, some fancied up with a feather in the band. Eve tried on several before finally settling for a pale beige with a plain brown band, setting it on her head at a rakish angle and grinning at her reflection. She looked a real cowgirl now! All she needed was the horse. The Circle Three carried a dozen or so, according to what Wade had told her. There was sure to be one she could appropriate for her own use.

A row of tooled leather boots caught her eye, but she didn't have enough cash on her. Another time, perhaps. If she was going to ride on a regular basis she was certainly going to need a pair. The insides of her calves already felt chafed from the rubbing of the stirrup leathers.

Back in the jeep again, she sat the hat more firmly on her head and switched on the ignition. It was only a little after one o'clock, yet she seemed to have packed so much into the day. Brett might even be back by now—not that she was going to allow that thought to dampen her spirits. She would even pay for the petrol she had used. No, *gas*, she corrected herself light-heartedly. If she was going to live this side of

the Atlantic she had better start embracing the
vernacular.

She made no effort to hurry her return to the
Diamond Bar, enjoying the sense of independence.
Adjusting to a climate like this one was no
hardship, although she was going to have to watch
herself for a few days until she started to acquire a
tan. A couple of hours sunbathing this afternoon
would give her a good start.

The main gates of the ranch were a good two
miles from the house. Still dragging it out, though
unwilling to admit it to herself, Eve brought the
jeep to a halt close by one of the waterholes,
running it off the road under the shade of a small
stand of trees. An old log half buried in the long
grass made a convenient perch at the water's edge.
Chewing a sweet stalk, she sat and watched the
teeming pond life, letting her thoughts drift
aimlessly. It was so peaceful here, so pleasantly
soothing out of the full heat of the sun. Another
half an hour wasn't going to make any difference
to anybody.

Half asleep, she never even heard the other
vehicle approaching—or if she did it was with the
very rim of consciousness. Her first intimation of
another presence was in the arm snaking roughly
about her waist from the rear, and by then it was
too late. Too shocked to cry out, she found herself
swung bodily up and backwards and was next
moment lying flat on her back in the long grass,
with every last ounce of breath crushed from her
by the weight of the hard male body.

CHAPTER FIVE

BRETT was wasting no time on verbal recriminations, his eyes glittering like diamonds as he brought his head down to find her mouth. There was no keeping her lips closed against him; he pressured them apart. His mouth was a weapon, thrusting ruthlessly through her defences, sending heat racing like fire through her veins. Every part of his body was moulded against her, his hips bearing down until her thighs buckled under the strain.

Somehow she tore her mouth free long enough to draw breath, almost hissing the words at him. 'Is *this* the only way you can make it?'

There were only two ways he could answer that jibe. For a moment it was touch and go, his hands already seeking the buckle of her belt. The effort of control was evidenced in the sudden clenching of his jaw, the narrowing of his eyes. For a long tense moment he looked down at her with fury still struggling to gain the upper hand, then he pushed himself upright, resting an elbow on one bent knee to rake a rough hand through his hair.

'You asked for it,' he gritted. 'You asked for a damned sight more!'

Eve had come to a sitting position too. It felt safer than back there in the grass. 'Why?' she asked recklessly. 'Because I refused to stick around like a good little girl and admire your rippling muscles? Sorry if you lost a little face with the boys, but I don't have to play up to your tin-god image!'

The skin about his mouth went white as his jaw tensed afresh. 'Why don't you quit while you're ahead?' he advised with dangerous softness.

Eve would have got to her feet were it not for the suspicion that any such move on her part might provoke him into losing the barely maintained control. She reached out instead and plucked another long blade of grass, registering the quiver in her fingers without surprise. She was in the wrong to a certain extent, but nothing she had done merited the savagery of that attack.

'You went to the Circle Three,' Brett said after a moment or two.

'After you'd told me not to. Yes, I know.' She paused, waiting for him to say something else, shrugging when he stayed silent. 'I didn't attempt to break into the house. As a matter of fact, I didn't even look through the windows. Wade showed me around, that's all.'

'Wade already?' The tone had an edge.

'You don't stand on ceremony in these parts, remember?' she said. 'It's all right, though. He calls *me* Boss.'

'You're pushing it!' he muttered between his teeth. 'You want putting on your back again, just keep that up!'

Hazel eyes met blue, the former dropping first. 'I apologise for taking the jeep,' Eve said huskily, 'but nothing else. How did you get back anyway?'

'I hitched a ride with Chuck on the truck. Once we finished the boys were too eager to get home to spend much time eating.' His tone was still brittle. 'You're going to have a lot of explaining to do to Fleur. She was spitting hair when I left!'

'I'm surprised she let you leave again without her.'

'She didn't have a choice. I wasn't in any mood for company.' He studied her grimly. 'I came close to doing something I wouldn't have been too proud of just now. If you'd gone straight back to the house I could have accepted it. Tracing you halfway across the county, then finding you sitting here without a care in the world—I just saw red, that's all. I've been doing it since you got here. What is it with you, Eve? Do you enjoy seeing how far you can push a guy before he cracks?'

She shook her head numbly. 'I went to the Circle Three because I wanted to go, not especially to defy you.' It wasn't easy to hold his gaze, but she made herself do it. 'Is there something wrong with the way Wade Connors handles his job?'

Dark brows drew together. 'What makes you think there might be?'

'The fact that you won't answer a straight question, for one thing,' she came back. 'I'm not stupid, Brett. The very mention of his name gets to you!'

His mouth had tightened again. 'He does his job okay.'

'Then it has to be personal.'

'If you say so.' He held up a staying hand as she started to speak. 'I'm not discussing it with you—now, or any other time.'

Personal *and* private, reflected Eve. It was more than remotely possible that a woman might be involved, she supposed. No doubt the girl back at the restaurant in town knew the story. Whether she ever got around to asking her was another matter.

'We should get back,' she said, and thought how hollow her voice sounded. 'They're going to wonder what happened.'

Brett reached out a hand as she started to get to her feet, pulling her down again. 'Not yet,' he stated. 'We still have a certain matter to take care of.'

Eve stared at him, her heart thudding painfully against the wall of her chest. 'I thought you'd already done that.'

'Not in the same sense.' The glitter was back in his eyes, but with a subtle difference. 'You asked me if that was the only way I could make it, didn't you? A question like that begs an answer.'

'I don't want . . .' she began, and saw his mouth take on the familiar slant.

'I'm not stupid either. Did you ever hear of *pheremones*?'

Eve shook her head, aware of the pulse beating so rapidly at her throat. 'Brett, I . . .'

'Broadly speaking, they're the subliminal scents released by animals at certain times.' His voice had taken on a new kind of depth, his eyes penetrating her defences without even trying. 'You're doing it right now, only with a woman it's more of an aura than a scent. Whichever, I'm not about to turn the invitation down. Not this time.'

She made no move to resist as he slid his fingers round the back of her neck to draw her to him, tremoring to the touch of his lips, feeling her willpower ebbing. He was right about the way she felt. She had known it the moment she had set eyes on him yesterday—and been moved to aggression because of it. Indulging a need, that was all it was. And why not? She had as much right to express her physical emotions as he did. With one difference, came the fleeting thought. Brett could take everything she had to offer and walk away unscathed. Could she?

The buttons of her shirt gave easily to his fingers, allowing him access to the warm flesh beneath. Still kissing her, he eased the garment back over her shoulders and down the length of her arms to fall clear, running a hand up her back to find the clip of her bra and expertly unfasten it; drawing the material away from her to bare her breasts to his erotic exploration.

If there had been any reticence at all in her it had vanished, body and mind totally committed. It was she herself who reached up to draw the dark head down to her, gasping at the sensuous rasp of his tongue over her tingling flesh. She didn't remember unfastening his shirt, only the dark curls of damp hair beneath her lips, the taste of salt in her mouth, the feel of his body pressing her back into the soft grass and the urgency of the hands tugging at her jeans.

The sudden sharp intake of breath and muffled groan brought little immediate comprehension. Only when Brett rolled abruptly away from her to lie on his back with eyes closed did the truth penetrate. The silence stretched between them like a tangible thread, tension quivering. Eve licked dry lips, bringing her own body under control by slow degrees. There was nothing she could say that would help ease the moment. All she could do was wait for Brett himself to initiate the next move.

When he did speak it was on a low rough note. 'I said last night nobody ever got to me as fast before. Don't judge the American male by that performance. It wasn't exactly typical.'

She said unhappily, 'It doesn't matter, Brett. I really didn't . . .'

'It damn well matters to me!' He sat up, lips

twisted. 'I never had it happen before. It takes some getting used to. For you too, I guess.'

It was a moment before Eve could gather herself to answer that one. 'Do I give the impression I have so much experience to draw on for comparison?' she asked at last, and saw his shoulders lift.

'You're not exactly inhibited when it comes to knowing what you want!'

'That doesn't necessarily suggest anything beyond the fact that I'm capable of like response.' She was pulling on her shirt as she spoke, trying not to hurry her actions. It was a little late now to start feeling selfconscious. 'Did you ever hear of instinct?'

'Sure.' His smile was humourless. 'Are you trying to tell me you're still a virgin?'

She said thickly, 'I'm telling you I'm not a tramp!'

'It never occurred to me you might be. Not that it's so important.' He started buttoning his own shirt, expression tightly controlled. 'We'd better get on back.'

Eve rose ahead of him, recognising the futility in trying to reach him. His pride had been stripped from him, and she had been witness. It was going to take him a long time to forgive her for that.

They reached the homestead in convoy, Brett in the lead. He pulled in at the gas pump, waving her on to the house itself. Fleur was sitting on the porch with Bart. She got to her feet as Eve brought the jeep to a stop, coming forward to the top of the step with a stormy expression.

'Have you been to the ranch?' she demanded. 'You had no right to go there without me!'

'I know, and I'm sorry. I should have called back for you first,' Eve acknowledged.

'If you hadn't gone off so quickly this morning I'd have been with you to start with,' pointed out her sister with indisputable logic. 'You never intended I should go, did you? You told Brett I wouldn't get up!'

'I told Brett I'd called you,' Eve came back with control, aware of Bart Hanson's presence at the other end of the porch. 'He wouldn't wait any later than six o'clock.'

'Only because you didn't ask him to. You didn't even bother coming back to make sure if I was up!'

Eve looked at her, brows faintly lifted. 'Were you?'

Fleur had the grace to blush a little. 'Well, no. I fell asleep again after you'd been in the first time. All the same . . .'

'All the same, you wouldn't have been in time.' Eve was past arguing the point any further. She needed to be alone. She attempted a smile. 'I'm going to have a shower and change my clothes. We can talk about it later.'

Fleur tossed her head, a petulant gesture hardly worthy of her age. 'I don't think we have anything to talk about. You're not going to change my mind about selling the Circle Three, Eve. If you want to hang on to it you're going to have to find half a million dollars to pay me my share, that's all.'

There was no reply to that—or none that Eve could think of immediately. Fleur was being difficult because she was angry, and she was angry because her pride had been hurt. It all came back to Brett in the end.

Bart was reading a newspaper with his back to them, obviously dissociating himself from this strictly family affair. 'We can't make any decision at all until Friday when we see Mr Shane,' she said. 'Even then it would hardly be an immediate transfer. We'd have to wait for the usual formalities connected with selling land.' She met stubborn brown eyes and sighed. 'Anyway, I'm going to have that shower.'

Her bedroom was a haven. It seemed a lot longer than a mere nine hours since she had left it. Her face had caught the sun, she noted dispassionately through the bathroom mirror as she stripped off her clothing. Luckily she tanned fairly easily. Tomorrow she was going to spend the whole day just lazing around, preparing herself mentally for whatever problems Friday was going to bring. Nothing else mattered but that.

It wasn't true, of course, she acknowledged wryly, stepping under the cool run of water. Right now the whole subject of the Circle Three had become of secondary importance. Facing Brett again was going to be difficult, not just because of what had happened to him, but because she herself had created the opportunity. She had known the man for little more than twenty-four hours all told. What kind of person did that make her? The feelings he aroused in her were involuntary, perhaps, but that didn't mean she had to give way to them. Where was her pride? What about self-respect? She had allowed Terry less in eighteen months than she had Brett in a day? Not that the latter would be coming near her again, she was certain. His own pride was going to take a lot of swallowing.

She was rinsing shampoo from her hair when the shower door opened at her back, and even as she started to turn a hand settled on her hipbone, propelling her further into the large cubicle. With hair streaming down over her face she heard the door close again and felt the presence of another naked body up close, then she was in Brett's arms and he was brushing aside the wet hair with his lips to find her mouth, his hands sliding down her back to lift her up to him.

'If I were thrown from a horse I'd get straight back on again,' he murmured thickly against her lips.

Eve tried desperately to press herself away from him, knowing even as she did so that it wasn't what she wanted to do, feeling the urge beating through her stronger and more forceful than before. The water raining down on them was a stimulant on its own, the shampoo still remaining on her hands and body transferring itself to his, robbing her of any real leverage. There was nowhere to go even if she could have torn herself free of him. He was between her and the door, his legs braced against movement, the droplets of water running down through the dark hair, glistening his skin the way it glistened hers. The feel of him against her undermined every moral fibre she possessed, husking her throat as she made one last faint plea. 'Brett, don't . . .'

'I have to,' he said. 'I need to.' His lips were at her temples, at her eyes, sliding downwards to the sensitive area just below her ear, the tip of his tongue spreading the moisture already there. The hands at her hips moved upwards over her body, following every curve until they reached her breasts, cupping the fullness in his palms while his thumbs slowly stroked her aching nipples.

With the pressure eased from the lower half of her body, Eve could have pulled away, but she didn't, her limbs softening to pliancy, hips beginning to move of their own accord, fingers hooking into the slippery muscles of his shoulders. She could hear his breath coming harder and faster even above the gushing noise of the water and the rising crescendo inside her head, but he was still in command. This time she was the one to break, stiffening against him with a moan torn from the very depths of her being.

'Now we start level,' he murmured.

Eve watched him reach out and turn off the tap with numbness creeping into her heart, standing stock still as he pushed open the door. He was smiling, his blue eyes full of assurance as they scanned her nude figure.

'I was right,' he said. 'You do have a lovely body.' He was stepping out of the cubicle as he spoke, taking one of the large fluffy towels from the rack and holding it up invitingly. 'Come on.'

Eve obeyed as if mesmerised, feeling the warmth enfold her, the firmness of his hands through the material as he dried her, the gathering of a new storm deep down inside.

'I thought you were going,' she murmured huskily, eyes closed. 'I thought . . .'

'I know what you thought.' Brett's own voice was low, his tone roughened. 'I guess that was the intention originally, only you changed my mind. We have a couple of hours before anybody's going to miss us—and we're going to make the most of them.'

She was beyond denying him—beyond anything but simply going along. Her hair was still wet when he lifted her up and carried her through to the other room to lay her on the bed, creating an instant damp patch on the pillow. She would have to dry it before Maria saw it, she found herself thinking with a part of her mind oddly detached from what was happening.

'The door,' she protested. 'Fleur might . . .'

'I locked it when I came in.' Brett was lying by her side on top of the covers, fingertips seeking the pulse beating so fast and hard at her throat for one fleeting moment before moving on slowly down to her breast. His head bent to follow that passage, his lips travelling over her skin with a lightness of touch that set every nerve end on fire. She clung to him mindlessly as he took one hardened nipple between his teeth, nails digging crescents in his flesh.

The world had receded, her every sense turned inward. Brett was drawing out time to its very limits, exploring her body with a leisurely enjoyment she could only return in kind. He carried no surplus flesh; her fingers could count each and every rib beneath the taut stretch of skin and muscle. She slid them around his waist to find his spinal column, following it downwards until her palms curved the firm male swell of his buttocks, feeling him move to cover her, his hand parting her thighs. He entered her slowly, penetrating deep and holding quite still for a long, long moment of sheer possessive power before beginning the rhythmic thrusting her body craved; building the pace until sight and sound and sensation itself blurred into one timeless void.

It was a long time before either of them could find either strength or desire to move. Lying there warm and drowsy under his weight, Eve had never felt more replete in her life. Reaction set in by degrees as memory returned to torment her. Two days ago she hadn't known this man existed, yet here she was in bed with him. No matter how wonderful an experience it had been, there was no getting away from bare fact.

'Not yet,' he said softly as he moved under him. 'Just stay the way you are. You feel good, Eve. Everything about you feels so good!' His lips brushed hers lightly, the blue eyes studying her face with a smile in their depths. 'I knew you were going to be trouble the minute I set eyes on you, only I guess I didn't realise just how much. You've given me a bad time, woman. I've a whole lot more compensation due!'

Her throat hurt. 'I have to go,' she got out. 'Let me up, Brett.'

He sighed once and rolled away from her. 'If you must you must. Just hurry back.'

Crossing the room naked under his gaze took all her courage—ridiculous, she knew, after what had passed between them, but it made little difference. His clothing lay in a heap just outside the bathroom door. She could visualise him standing there after entering the room, listening to the sound of the shower and deciding on his course of action. He had obviously not been prepared to accept a rejection easily, yet that was small comfort. She had made it too easy.

With the door closed between them, she stood for a moment or two trying to gather herself together. The lingering, pleasurable ache in her body was a reminder she couldn't ignore. It was a little too late for regrets, anyway. What had happened had happened; there was no going back. The thing to think about now was how she handled the situation from here on in. Brett was waiting for her to go back to him out there, confident in the assumption that she would be only too willing. So far as her physical reactions were concerned, he assumed correctly. It was her emotional state she found so difficult to unravel. Yesterday's antipathy had been a cover-up for attraction, that she had to admit. One glance was all it had taken. Everything she had said or done since had been calculated to make him take notice of her; she had to be honest about that too. If she had succeeded rather too well then that was her own fault, not his.

None of which helped at this moment, she acknowledged wryly. Whatever her feelings for Brett, the Circle Three still loomed between them. He wanted that land too badly to give it up. And if she gave it up, what then? If her own involvement was rather more than merely physical, his was almost certainly not so. She would be sacrificing everything she held dear for a transient affair. No matter how superb a lover he might be, the price was far too high.

She wrapped a towel sarong-style around her before returning to the bedroom, loth to put on the clothes she had worn all day. Brett was lying on his stomach in an attitude of total relaxation, head turned sideways and eyes closed. Even in repose his body had no slackness about it, the flat muscle clearly visible under the deeply tanned skin of his back, his thighs fined and strengthened by years of straddling a saddle. One arm hung limply over the side of the bed, the fingers slightly curled.

'Don't stand there like a dummy,' he said suddenly, still without opening his eyes. 'I'm just gathering strength.'

'You're wasting your time.' Her voice was as unemotional as she could make it. 'I want you to go, Brett.'

It was a moment before he moved. When he did it was without haste, rolling over on to his side to look at her with narrowed eyes. 'Why?' he demanded. 'You got as much out of it as I did.'

'I'm not saying I didn't.' She clutched the towel tighter about her, hanging on to her composure with the same desperation. 'You came here to prove something. Well, you proved it.'

'Because you let me?'

'No, not because I let you. I couldn't have stopped you.' She paused, biting her lip, but said it anyway. 'I didn't want to stop you.'

There was no change of expression on the lean features. 'So where's the problem? We're two adult people, Eve—at least, I'd have said so. If it's soft words and romantic declarations you're after, you came to the wrong man. I'm no good at that sort of thing.' The admission held no shadow of regret. 'I want you; I know you feel the same way. Where we go from here remains to be seen.'

'What about the Circle Three?' she asked softly. 'Do you still intend trying to buy it?'

He studied her for a long moment, eyes hardening a fraction. 'Sure,' he said. 'That has nothing to do with this.'

'It has to have some bearing,' she protested. 'I can't fight you on one level and make love on another!' She paused again, her breath coming hard and heavy as she met the vivid gaze. 'Or were you anticipating a change of mind on my part?'

His laugh sounded harsh. 'You underestimate yourself, honey. Buying land was the last thing on my mind when I came in that shower with you, believe me!'

Eve did believe it; the memory alone scorched her mind. 'That was this time,' she said. 'I'm not making any excuses for what happened, but neither can I pretend to be what I'm not. I can't handle the kind of affair you have in mind, Brett. It's as simple as that.'

He didn't answer right away, his regard steady but unrevealing. 'Fleur told me you had a very close boy-friend back home,' he said at length. 'What kind of relationship was that?'

Eve sat down in the nearby chair, her knees too weak to hold her upright any longer. 'I was in love with him,' she said. 'Or I thought I was, which amounts to the same thing.'

'And you have to be in love with a man before you can make love?' The tone was very soft.

Her eyes lifted, holding his firmly. 'I think I just proved that isn't necessarily true. I don't even know you very well—and what I do know I'm not sure I like all that much.'

His mouth tilted. 'You're not giving either of us much credit, are you? What is it you don't like about me?'

'You don't give a damn,' she responded levelly, 'so why bother asking?'

This time the smile was genuinely amused. 'You could have something there, though you're the first female I've met capable of seeing it. Okay, so you don't have to like me. As to knowing me better . . .' he shrugged . . . 'it takes time. Cutting out any contact between us isn't going to hasten the process any.'

'There's contact and contact,' she came back, steeling herself to follow the same line. 'The kind you have in mind is too temporary anyway.'

'Who said anything about temporary?' He got up from the bed in one lithe movement, coming towards her without haste, eyes glinting as the colour flooded her cheeks. 'You're a curious mixture,' he murmured softly, pulling her to her feet. 'Wild as they come in bed, yet still embarrassed by nudity outside of it. I'm going to change all that, Eve. I'm going to enjoy getting rid of all those hidden inhibitions of yours. We'll sort our differences some other time.'

She was being a fool, and she knew it, yet knowing it made little impact on the emotions burning through her. She felt the towel drop from her, the heat and hardness of him enveloping her, then all coherent thought was gone.

CHAPTER SIX

THE plane bringing the lawyer down from Orlando came in just after four on the Friday afternoon. Alec Shane proved to be a mild-mannered man in his early sixties, his conservative dark suit and rimless spectacles congruous with his profession. Bart greeted him with familiarity, introducing him to the two girls the same way.

'Brett's out at the sheds right now,' he said, after seeing his new guest seated with a cool drink to hand. 'He'll be another hour or so maybe.'

'Plenty of time,' the other man responded easily. 'I'm planning on staying overnight.' He sat back in the cane chair with a small sigh of pleasure. 'It's always good to get away from the office for a spell—especially to visit the Diamond Bar! One or two things I need to talk over with you, too, Bart. If we could get through before dinner I can devote the greater part of the evening to Circle Three affairs.' The last with a smile for both girls. 'I have the detailed valuation with me, if you're at all interested in going through it. Not that it's necessary—all I really need is your signatures on the bill of sale. You brought along the documentation I asked for, of course?'

Eve confirmed that they had, conscious of Fleur's stony silence. The atmosphere between them had been strained for the past two days, with little she could do about it. Whether her sister suspected the truth where Brett was concerned, she wasn't sure. Certainly her whole attitude towards him had altered.

And what about her own attitude? She reflected wryly as the two men became involved in conversation. Both Wednesday night and last night Brett had come to her room, ignoring the fact that Fleur was right next door, and making her ignore it too. No matter how often she vowed to finish what they had begun, he only had to touch her and she was lost. Already her own involvement had gone beyond the point of retreat, her interests so divided she could no longer be sure of what she wanted any more. There had been no further mention of the Circle Three, yet that didn't mean Brett had changed his ideas at all. In fact, she doubted if the thought had even crossed his mind. Alex Shane had come here prepared to complete the whole transaction in one fell swoop. That had to be with Brett's full knowledge. While it had not previously occurred to her that Aunt Laura and the Hansons might share the same legal adviser, there was nothing basically wrong in that. Conspiracy was just a word in her mind. No one looking at Alex Shane could for an instant imagine him capable of anything even mildly unorthodox when it came to exercising his professional arm.

What she had to ask herself was where the future lay. Brett wanted her now, but what about next month—or even next week? He had told Fleur they were welcome to stay on at the Circle Three homestead as long as they liked, only Fleur herself might no longer want to do that. Could she do it alone? Eve wondered. Could she wait there for Brett to come to her, never knowing how long it was going to last? Or was she being too pessimistic about the whole affair? Wasn't it just possible that Brett himself might find his deeper emotions becoming involved given time?

Refusal to agree to the sale was hardly likely to bring them closer, that she had to acknowledge. Nor was it going to make Fleur happy. She could finish up losing both of them in the end. Did she really want to take that risk?

Dinner was the usual informal meal, with all three men casually clad in slacks and shirts. Eve forced an air of insouciance, knowing even while she chatted so brightly that Brett was not deceived for a moment. Each time she caught his eye he was watching her with the same faint, ironic smile on his lips, as if he could read every passing thought in her mind.

It was Alex Shane himself who suggested they make a start on legal affairs, and Bart who insisted they use the study for privacy. Eve had seen the room only fleetingly in passing. It was a purely male domain, the desk huge and heavy, the leather chairs comfortably shabby. Seated in one of them, Eve smiled across at Fleur, but the latter simply stared through her, no expression whatsoever in her eyes. They were strangers, and it was her fault, Eve thought numbly. The least she could do was give her sister the consolation of hard cash.

The file Alex Shane took from his briefcase was thick and heavy. He spread papers from it in meticulous order across the desk, resting his elbows on the surface and making a steeple of his fingers as he looked at the two waiting faces.

'I think the best way to start is to try and put the whole thing in a nutshell,' he said. 'After that you can ask any questions you need to ask.' He took their agreement for granted, clearing his throat before continuing. 'The land itself is naturally the most valuable part of the ranch, although the stock and machinery should fetch a fair price on the open market. At a thousand dollars an acre, Brett is being more than generous. After all, the land is almost totally enclosed within Diamond Bar boundaries. The only way any outsider might be tempted to buy the whole ranch as a going concern would be on the strength of profits, which hardly apply to the Circle Three anyway.'

'I'm not sure I understand,' Eve broke in confusedly. 'You're saying the ranch isn't a profitable concern?'

'Well, no. It's been barely paying its way the past ...' the lawyer paused to consult one of his papers, pushing his spectacles further up his nose ... 'eight or nine years. It was viable once, of course, when beef prices were sky-high. By today's demands it's too small a concern to stay afloat on profits. Fortunately the income itself wasn't important. Your uncle kept it going purely and simply because it had been in the family for so long.' He smiled a little. 'And, I fancy, because he cherished his image as a landowner. He could have chosen to live in far more luxurious style, but it wasn't what he wanted. Neither did your aunt. They were a very contented couple. She never really got over his death. She carried on running the Circle Three—with the Hansons' help—in his memory, for no other reason. Even when she became too ill to take an active part, she used to have Brett go over the figures with her every month, just to be sure the books were up to date the way Jos would have liked them—and to make up any deficit. Some people may call that sending good money after bad.' The smile came again. 'I have to confess to a certain reluctance to condone the practice on my own part. Her financial advisers tried every way they could to persuade her to sell out, until Bart made them leave her alone. She was staying right here in this house by then, so he was able to monitor her calls.'

Fleur spoke for the first time since they had come into the room, her voice almost hushed. 'Are you saying there's a lot more money, apart from what the land is worth?'

'That's a very simplified way of putting it,' the lawyer responded, 'but yes, in essence, that's quite correct. You have to realise, of course, that your capital is tried up in investments of various kinds. They're all down here if you'd like to go over them. The accountants don't advise any changes at present time, although they'll naturally be in touch themselves to discuss the matter. After deduction of taxes, your income will be in the region of ...' once again he paused to consult a paper, taking what seemed to be an eon of time ... 'four hundred and eighty thousand dollars a year. Two hundred and forty thousand each, if you intend to split the figure equally down the middle. That doesn't take into any account the capital from the land sale. Invested ...' He spread his hands. 'All I can say is you'll both be very wealthy young ladies.'

The silence after he had finished speaking could be felt. Eve was motionless, too stunned to take it all in.

'Why us?' she got out at length. 'Aunt Laura didn't even know us!'

'You were the only relatives she had left in the world,' the lawyer explained. 'She always regretted not having kept in better touch with her family. "Young people are the only ones who know how to enjoy money," she said to me once. I wouldn't totally agree with her judgment, but her sentiments were sound.'

'I know exactly what she meant!' Fleur was sitting on the extreme edge of her seat, eyes sparkling, her whole face alive. 'You can do what you like about the ranch, Eve. I think I can manage quite well on the rest! How long will it be?' The last to Alec Shane.

'Before you can start spending it?' There was just a hint of irony in the question. 'No time at all. All I need is your joint signatures, plus notarisation of the birth certificates you brought with you. I've already made arrangements for accounts to be opened at the bank in Leesville for immediate expenses. The manager there will be expecting you over in the morning to identify yourselves.'

'You never mentioned any of this in your letter,' said Eve, still not wholly recovered from the initial shock. 'We had the impression the ranch was all there was.'

'My first communication was only intended to convey the fact of the legacy itself,' came the mild reply. 'I mentioned the offer for the land merely because it happened to be a solid figure I had at my fingertips. After you rang and told me you were coming over in person it was obviously simpler to hold everything in abeyance until you arrived.'

'What does it matter anyway?' asked Fleur dismissively. 'What does *any*thing matter now!'

Was Brett included in there? wondered Eve, trying to see beyond the brightness in her sister's face. She hoped so, if only to still her conscience where he was concerned. That aspect of their relationship was not the only one bothering her at the moment, however. She had a battle to fight within herself.

'About the land?' said the lawyer, almost as if he read her thoughts. 'Do I take it there's some difference of opinion between the two of you regarding the sale?'

'Eve wants to live there and run the ranch herself,' put in Fleur before Eve could answer. 'I was against it before I knew what I know now, but ...' she paused, lifting her shoulders in a pretty little shrug, her smile humouring her sister's whims ... 'if that's what she wants to do I'm not going to be greedy about it!'

The eyes behind the spectacles had not left Eve's face. 'You realise you'll have to go on subsidising the ranch out of your own income?'

'Yes.' Her voice sounded far away; she made an effort to concentrate. 'Yes, I do.'

'But you still intend to go ahead?'

'Yes.' This time her voice was stronger, the decision instinctive rather than rationally thought out. 'For a time, at any rate.' She looked back at him with determination in her eyes. 'I know it must sound crazy to you, but I have to.'

His shrug was philosophical. 'No crazier than a lot of other schemes I hear of. You can afford it. Why not?' He briskened again. 'There are one or two other minor matters to take care of before we complete. For instance ...'

Eve listened with only half an ear, wondering how she was going to tell Brett that he wasn't getting the land he coveted so dearly—numbly calculating the odds against retaining his regard in any sphere. To live without it wasn't going to be easy, yet how long would it have lasted in any case?' This way she had a base, a place to set down roots. Fleur would no doubt want to travel and see something of the rest of the country, if not the world, but she would also need a place to come back to from time to time. The Circle Three would be right there waiting.

Bart was watching television on his own when they finally returned to the living room. He switched off the set and swung his chair, his glance going from Fleur's excited, glowing face to Eve's comparative pallor with some comprehension.

'Brett went down to the dispensary,' he said. 'They had to call in the vet to a sick calf. Anyone like a drink?'

Eve had a brandy; she needed it to help steady her nerves. 'When shall we be able to move over to the Circle Three?' she asked Alex Shane a little later.

'As soon as you like,' he said. 'I believe the house needs some attention.'

'Wade Connors said one of the ranch wives would help with the cleaning.' She sent a small apologetic smile in Bart's direction. 'Please don't think I haven't been grateful for all your hospitality. It was good of you to put us up.'

'Think nothing of it. I've enjoyed the company.' He paused, watching her with an odd expression. 'I hope you'll still come and visit pretty often.'

'Of course,' she said. 'We're only going to be a few miles away.'

'Not me!' exclaimed Fleur with blissful satisfaction. 'I'm going to fly down to Miami and buy some super clothes, then book myself on a Caribbean cruise. And that's just for starters! I can live the kind of life I've only read about up till now, and nobody to tell me any different. It's going to be just wonderful!'

Eve caught Bart's eye and bit back the words trembling on her lips. He was right, of course. Fleur was of an age to make her own mistakes. One could only hope they wouldn't be too traumatic.

Brett didn't return to the house until after eleven. He looked tried, his shirt clinging damply to his chest and back.

'We lost the calf,' he said briefly. 'Mike's coming out in the morning to do a P.M. If it's what he thinks it is we're going to have to vaccinate the whole herd.' His glance rested a bare moment on Eve before moving on to Alex Shane. 'Sorry about this. Are you going to be able to stay over the weekend?'

The lawyer smiled. 'I don't have anything to rush back for.'

'Good, then I'm going to turn in, if nobody minds. It could be a heavy day.'

None of them lingered long after that. Fleur went off to her room still floating on cloud nine. Showered, and in her thin cotton nightdress, Eve opened a window, turning off the air-conditioning as she did so. The early evening rain shower had brought out a whole host of new scents to tantalise her nostrils as well as cooling the atmosphere. The faint breeze felt so good on her skin.

She was still standing there when the door opened behind her. Brett closed it again as she turned. He was wearing the short black silk robe which was his only concession to bedroom apparel, his feet bare.

'Time all good girls were in bed,' he said softly.

Eve didn't move. 'I thought you'd turned in for the night,' she said. 'I didn't expect you.'

He smiled a little. 'I couldn't sleep. That's how far you've gotten hold!' He came across to her, putting both hands under the line of her jaw to tilt her face to his lingering kiss. 'Come and satisfy my baser instincts,' he murmured, 'your own inimitable way!'

'Brett, there's something we have to talk about,' Eve got out, fighting the urge to let it go for the moment. 'You may not want . . .'

'If you're trying to tell me you're not going to let me have the Circle Three, you don't have to bother,' he came back, dry-toned. 'Your face said it all when I came in from the dispensary. What does that have to do with here and now?'

She gazed at him in confusion, trying to read the mind behind the vivid eyes. 'You don't care?'

'Sure I care. I still want that land.' He hadn't released her, his fingers caressing the taut skin of her throat. 'There's time yet. Situations can change—people can change.'

Or be changed, she thought. There was more than one kind of persuasion. She put up her hands and caught his, staying the motion. Her voice sounded thick in her ears. 'It won't work, Brett. I don't care whether it lacks common sense or not, I'm going to keep the ranch going. I'm sorry Aunt Laura gave you false hopes, but she can't really have wanted it to happen or she would have done something about it.'

He was studying her with an odd expression, his fingers still beneath hers. 'You believe if she said it at all she was only fobbing me off, is that it?'

Her own gaze didn't falter. 'Yes.'

There was a momentary pause before his features relaxed, his mouth taking a faint slant. 'It's an improvement on being called an out-and-out liar, at any rate. Anything else to get off your chest before we get back to more pressing matters?'

Eve shook her head, relief flooding her. 'I thought it would finish us,' she admitted.

'But you intended going ahead with it anyway.' There was a certain wry quality in his voice. 'Maybe you haven't been getting as much out of this last couple of days as you make out.'

'You don't really believe that.' She was smiling, her mouth soft with the memory of all that had passed between them. 'You know exactly what you can make me feel.'

Brett's own smile was slow. 'Suppose you try convincing me with some tangible evidence? *Show* me what I make you feel, Eve.'

There was still a certain reticence in her initial response to that challenge, her fingers all thumbs as she unfastened the tie belt of his robe and slid her hands over the taut flesh beneath, following the line of muscle and sinew with a touch that brought a sudden groan to his lips.

Removal of her nightdress was a simple matter of sliding both shoulders straps down over her arms and allowing the garment to fall to the floor about her ankles. Eve stepped out of it without thinking about it, her lips seeking the velvety warmth of him, cherishing each point of contact, sensing the tension mounting inside him until it reached the point where he could take no more, his hands pressing her down to the floor beneath him.

'Damn you,' he growled when the room finally steadied again, 'you learn too fast!'

Too fast for her own good, Eve acknowledged with a sudden depressing descent into reality. Her emotions were too deeply entangled to be cut loose without pain. All she could hope for was Brett's own eventual entrapment in the same toil.

The bank manager's greeting was respectful without being over-effusive, large accounts obviously of no particular rariety in this part of the world. Within moments they had been issued with cheque books and a multitude of credit cards already applied for in their respective names. There were few actual cash transactions in the U.S.A., the sisters learned; most companies preferred accounts backed by a reliable source.

Out in the sunlit main street again, Alex Shane eyed the area of cloud rearing up from the western horizon and calculated that they had a couple of hours before it rained. Time, he said, to see the homestead itself and organise some help in cleaning up the house. Eve's acknowledgment of her previous visit was received without censure.

'No real reason why you shouldn't have gone alone,' he said easily. 'The law isn't that rigid.'

'Brett seemed to think so,' put in Fleur as she climbed back into the station wagon. 'He told us we weren't to set foot on the place before you arrived.'

The lawyer smiled at her through the driving mirror. 'He probably wasn't feeling too happy about the whole situation at the time. Put yourself in his position: he'd taken it for granted that Laura had kept her word.'

Eve said softly, 'Did she ever really intend to put that clause in the will?'

Alex hesitated, fingers on the ignition key. 'She certainly talked about it. She just never got around to doing anything concrete about it, that's all. In the end she was too ill to even think about legal matters, although she went peacefully enough owing to the care she received from all quarters. She was very happy living with the Hansons. She trusted them.'

It was Eve's turn to smile. 'You don't have to underline that fact. I might have harboured some suspicions regarding motivation when I first arrived, but things weren't as clear.'

'She means,' said Fleur from the rear, 'that she didn't feel the same way about Brett at the time.' There was just the barest hint of malice in the tone. 'Things are different now, aren't they, Eve?'

Aware of Alex's swift glance, Eve fought to retain her composure. 'I believe what he tells me, yes,' she agreed on a light note. 'I was wrong to react the way I did—I admit it.'

'Everyone makes mistakes,' rejoined Alex, putting the vehicle into motion. 'Recognition is the main thing.'

Fleur didn't speak again on the way out to the Circle Three, leaving Eve to wonder just how far she really was over Brett. Last night the thought of all that money had filled her entire mind to the exclusion of everything else, this morning, with the shock absorbed to a certain extent, she could begin to consider other emotional needs. The sooner the air was cleared between them the better, Eve decided, though what exactly she was going to tell her was a matter to ponder. Not even to Fleur could she bring herself to acknowledge her deeper feelings, yet to leave them out of the affair left it looking exactly that—a casual liaison, purely physical on both sides.

The rain came sooner than Alex had anticipated, drumming a staccato rhythm on the roof of the car as they turned in through the ranch gates. He brought them to a halt as close to the house as he could get, jumping out with a surprising agility for a man his age and bounding up the broad step on to the covered verandah to put a key to the front door lock.

'Better make a run for it if you don't want to sit there for half an hour till it lets up,' he called. 'You can be looking through the house meantime.'

Both girls slid from their seats in unison, banging the doors and darting across the narrow gap of open ground to arrive laughing and rain-spotted beneath the protecting roof.

'At least it's warm rain,' gasped Fleur, shaking the sparkling droplets from her hair.

'And it rarely lasts long,' agreed the lawyer. 'The sun will be out again before you know it.'

'You don't have to sell us on the climate,' Eve responded smilingly. 'We're already convinced—at least, I certainly am!'

There was no reply from Fleur, who had moved on ahead of them into the house. Eve followed slowly with Alec at her back, taking in the dust-sheeted furnishings and drape-covered windows of the large room opening out from the entrance hallway. There was a stillness about the place, a sense of time suspended. A woman she had never even known had lived here, loved here, laughed, and no doubt sometimes even cried here. She could almost feel her presence, not oppressive but friendly and welcoming.

'There shouldn't be very much needs doing to get the place ready for occupation again,' declared the lawyer, walking across the stretch of off-white carpeting to draw back silky gold drapes from floor-to-ceiling glass doors. 'Luckily it won't be standing empty through another summer's humidity. That's the time when deterioration sets in.'

Fleur had followed him across, looking out through the glass at the lawned and paved yard area with delight. 'A pool!' she exclaimed. 'You never told me there was a pool, Eve!'

Eve shook her head. 'I didn't get round to the back of the house. Wade just showed me round the outbuildings and talked about general running.' She was pleased herself. 'It's going to be lovely to have a dip whenever we feel like it.'

'Laura felt that way too,' acknowledged Alex, smiling at their reaction. 'We don't notice the heat so much ourselves, but she never really acclimatised to the summers out here. Come and see the rest of the house. It isn't quite as big as the Hansons' place, but Jos had a hand in the design himself when they rebuilt the old homestead, and he was no mean architect.'

It was easy to see that for themselves. From the four bedrooms, each with its own bathroom and walk-in closet, down through the beautifully equipped and spacious kitchen to the living and dining areas overlooking the pool and rear flower gardens, the whole house was immaculate. It had a good atmosphere, even Fleur was bound to admit. One could tell that the people who had lived here had been happy the vast majority of their time.

'We'll take it,' Eve quipped as they came back to the hallway. 'How soon can we move in?'

Alex lifted his shoulders. 'It's up to you. The beds will need making up, of course, and there has to be a lot of dust around even though everything has been sheeted. Depends on how soon someone is willing to come in. You shouldn't have any difficulty finding staff. Laura used to insist on doing all the cooking herself, but you may feel differently about it.'

'I enjoy cooking,' Eve admitted. 'Help with the cleaning would be appreciated, though. I . . .' She broke off as a shadow fell across the opened doorway, a smile of recognition crossing her face at the sight of the tall, fair-haired man standing on the threshold. 'Hallo there!'

Wade Connors was smiling too, one hand resting lightly against the jamb. 'I saw the car— thought you might need a hand. Everything okay?'

'Fine,' Fleur said smoothly before Eve could answer, deliberately drawing his attention away from her sister. 'Just perfect, in fact.' Her eyes were riveted to the handsome features. 'You must be Wade. I'm Fleur Brockley.'

He grinned, expression unashamedly appreciative. 'Pleased to meet you, ma'am,' he drawled in lightly mocking mimicry of a certain movie star. 'Anything at all you want to know, I'm your man.'

'It's stopped raining,' she said. 'Why don't you show me round? After all, Eve's already seen everything.'

'A pleasure.' Briefly his eyes sought Eve's. 'I lined up Jenny Hackney and Marnie Grayson for the cleaning out. They'll come in on a regular basis if you want them.'

'That sounds good,' she acknowledged. Fleur's response to this man was a relief in itself. If she were still harbouring any feelings at all for Brett, she was obviously more than prepared to find room for Wade Connors. It wouldn't last, of course, any more than any of Fleur's interests lasted. On the other hand, there was every chance that Wade might prove a big enough attraction to make her forget about Miami and that cruise for a while. Alone, she would be ripe pickings for any good-looking fortune-hunter who happened along.

She and Alex Shane conducted their own tour of the immediate premises, chatting with a couple of the men at work round the barns in passing and assuring them that no jobs were going to be lost.

'It's your money,' Alec stated more than once as if in mitigation of his own position. 'Your income can stand it. Just providing this is really what you want to do.'

Eve assured him it was. If a shadow of doubt remained in her mind at all it was only because she foresaw a time when Brett would not be prepared to put their relationship before his longer-standing needs. She would cross that bridge when she came to it, she told herself, and knew she was only delaying the inevitable.

CHAPTER SEVEN

It was an hour or more before Wade brought Fleur back to the car where the other two waited.

'Sorry if I held you up,' he apologised easily. 'We got talking and time just went, I guess.'

'I really enjoyed it,' said Fleur. Her eyes were on Eve, the expression in them faintly disturbing. 'I'm looking forward to coming to live here. It's a super place!'

Wade was smiling. 'When can we expect you?'

'How does tomorrow sound?' responded Eve. 'We're both quite capable of turning to when it comes to getting things shipshape.'

'You speak for yourself,' said Fleur. 'The first thing I'm going to do when we get here is plunge into the pool!' Her glance shifted back to Wade, taking on a certain sparkle in the process. 'We'll have a pool party, seeing it's the weekend. Everyone's invited! We can barbecue some steaks on the grid out there.'

'I'll send one of the boys into town this afternoon,' Wade promised. 'The kitchen needs restocking anyway. We'll be there, miss.'

'It's Fleur,' she said. 'I told you to call me Fleur.'

'Will do.' He nodded to Eve. 'See you in the morning, then. I'll get the girls to work right away.'

'He's out of this world!' Fleur exclaimed as the car drew away a moment or two later. 'With a face like that he should be in films!'

'Faces like his are ten a penny in Hollywood,' Alex put in dryly. 'Anyway, his life is out here running the Circle Three.'

'He wouldn't be doing it if Brett had his way,' came the response from the rear on a suddenly cool note. 'Wade says he planned on clearing the whole area for grazing—including the house.'

'Wade says' was going to become a regular phrase until the novelty wore off, Eve suspected wryly. When Fleur switched her attentions she did it wholesale. 'I can't believe that,' she said on a mild note. 'Brett wouldn't knock down a lovely place like that just to gain him a few hundred feet of extra grazing land.'

'There was a time not so very long ago when you thought him capable of just about anything,' her sister came back. There was a slight pause before she added pointedly, 'Perhaps first impressions were the right ones after all.'

Eve twisted in her seat to look back at the bland face. 'Is that supposed to mean something?'

'Depends how you look at it.' Fleur was by no means put down by the sharp demand. 'I learned a few things about friend Brett this morning.'

'Connors isn't what I'd call an unprejudiced witness,' said Alex, sounding uncomfortable. 'If he and Brett have gotten across one another it has to be for a good reason.'

'I'm sure.' Fleur was enjoying herself, a flicker of malice in her eyes. 'Wade knows something Brett would prefer kept secret—that's a very good reason.'

'I think you should shut up about it,' Eve advised, trying to keep her tone level. 'Whatever happened between the two of them, it's their affair, not ours.'

Fleur shrugged. 'You might change your mind when you hear the story.'

'Except that I don't want to hear it.' This time Eve made no attempt to keep the anger from her voice. 'Drop it, will you!'

Fleur dropped it, the petulant look creeping back about her pretty mouth. People didn't speak to her that way—particularly not her own sister! Conscious of the heavy atmosphere, Eve made some casual comment to Alex about the house they had just left, to have him gratefully seize on the new topic. Family arguments were anathema to those outside them.

Despite her injunction to Fleur, she found herself unable to put the matter out of her mind. If Wade Connors really had some kind of hold over Brett then surely his job would have been in no danger at all? That he had told Fleur some story was obvious, yet it was all too possible that she was deliberately exaggerating. Brett was not forgiven for his lack of response; what she was looking for was a rod to beat him with. Perhaps the best way of handling things was to listen to just what it was that Wade had told her and then try to put matters into perspective. From past experience she knew that simply leaving the subject to simmer in her sister's mind was asking for trouble.

They reached the Diamond Bar in time for lunch. Brett wasn't present, although Bart was able to tell them that the threatened epidemic was not about to materialise after all. He received the news of their impending move with unconcealed regret. He'd enjoyed the companionship these last few days, he admitted to Eve.

'It's only a few miles,' she pointed out. 'I'm

going to take up riding on a regular basis once I find a suitable horse, so I'll be coming over most days.'

'Laura had a chestnut mare she set great store by,' Bart responded. 'So far as I know, she's still on the stock list. Could be a bit of a handful for a relative beginner if she's been out to grass for the last year, though. Might be better to start fresh.'

'I'll see,' Eve agreed. She liked the idea of riding her aunt's own favourite.

As Alex had predicted, the sun was as hot as ever after the rain. Eve took a magazine out on to the rear terracing after lunch, knowing Fleur would probably follow her.

She was not disappointed. The latter came out some fifteen minutes later, throwing herself down on a long cane chair with a sigh of pure pleasure.

'I shan't have any trouble at all taking to this life,' she declared. 'No washing up, no making beds!'

Since when had she done either? thought Eve with an inward smile. Her own fault, of course, except that doing it oneself was so much easier than constantly nagging someone else.

'If you've got something to tell me,' she said, 'you'd better get it off your chest. You'll never rest until you have.'

The vivacious features took on a resentful look. 'Don't indulge me, Eve!'

'I'm sorry.' The penitence was genuine. 'Is it so important?'

'Yes, it is. You'll think so too when you know.' She was slightly mollified but still on the offensive. 'Your precious Brett isn't what you think he is. Not by a long chalk!'

'He was *your* precious Brett too for a couple of

days,' Eve pointed out mildly. 'Are you sure this isn't sour grapes to a certain extent?'

'Because you wormed your way in with him?' The blonde head moved in emphatic denial. 'I saw through him before that. He's a complete fraud. He doesn't have any feelings for anyone except himself and what *he* wants!'

'Keep your voice down.' Eve spoke in low tones herself, aware of the opened windows and carrying quality of her sister's accents. 'You're making very strong accusations on the strength of some tale from a man you don't even know.'

'Wade didn't want to tell me. I wormed it out of him.'

And who opened the subject to start with? wondered Eve, but she refrained from asking the question. 'So get on with it,' she said. 'Let's have it out in the open where we can look at it—let's hope, without prejudice, as they say in the courts!'

The weak joke failed to raise a smile. She hadn't really expected it to do so. Fleur obviously felt strongly enough about this whole affair to have lost any sense of humour.

'How would you feel about a man,' the latter said slowly, 'who had an affair with his own stepmother?'

The pause was long and fraught. Eve could hear a bird calling somewhere out in the shrubbery, but the sound seemed to come from a long distance. When she did find her voice it could have belonged to a total stranger. 'I wouldn't believe it,' she said flatly.

Fleur shrugged. 'It's up to you, only you can hardly doubt visual evidence.'

'Meaning what?'

'Meaning Wade saw the two of them together.'

'So he saw them together.' Eve was fighting to retain a rational viewpoint. 'What does that prove, beyond the fact that they got along well enough to want to be in each other's company?'

'Are you being deliberately dense?' demanded her sister with impatience. 'He saw them *together!* Making love, if you want it spelling out for you.'

'I don't need anything spelling out for me.' Eve could feel the quiver deep down inside, the sensation of something hard and hurtful beginning to unfurl barbed little points. 'He could have been mistaken.'

'Not in the circumstances. They'd been out riding, and Wade almost rode over them in the grass down by the river. Brett's had it in for him ever since. He even tried to poison Aunt Laura's mind against him. Luckily Aunt Laura was too fond of him to listen. Wade was like a son to her.'

'His opinion or hers?' Eve asked bitingly. She caught her lower lip between her teeth at the look in Fleur's eyes. 'All right, I'll accept that. It's the opinion I formed myself the first time we spoke.'

'And you accept that Wade isn't the kind to make up a story like that just out of spite?' Fleur insisted.

Eve shook her head. 'About that I wouldn't know. I'll grant he doesn't seem the type.' She was succeeding in keeping the hurt contained, refusing to allow it rein without further cause than this. 'He could have been mistaken. Perhaps they were just sitting talking.'

'Oh, come off it! They were practically undressed. Wade says Brett must have been doing the persuading, because Diane was actually struggling to get away from him.'

'That's pure supposition! He can't possibly have

known what was in her mind at the time—unless he asked her?'

'I doubt it. He didn't like her.'

'Maybe he tried to make her too, and was turned down.'

'No!' Fleur's face had coloured hotly. 'You don't have any right to say that!'

There was a momentary pause before Eve inclined her head. 'You're right, I don't. Only it's one man's word against another's, isn't it?'

'If Brett denies it, yes, I suppose it is.' Fleur waited a deliberate moment before saying it. 'Dare you ask him?'

'I haven't any business asking him.'

'If you haven't I don't know who has.' The smile had an edge. 'After all, he is your lover.' She met the swift upward glance without a flicker. 'Did you really think I didn't know? I've heard him come to your room at night.'

The wave of heat was uncontrollable. 'You've listened?'

'Not deliberately. The walls are thick enough to cut out all but the faintest sound of voices. It's just that I didn't see you carrying out an ordinary conversation at two o'clock in the morning.' Fleur waited, studying her sister's face with a certain satisfaction. 'I'm not condemning you for it, even if it was a bit quick. I'll bet he's great in bed!'

Eve took a grip on herself. 'That's not your affair.'

'Neither was the other, if you put it that way,' came the prompt and totally unperturbed response. 'It has to be yours, though, unless you don't mind what he got up to before you met him. After all, what's a stepmother or two? She can't have been all that much older than him, I suppose. Some men can't resist older women, they say. It doesn't really hold out very much hope for you, though, does it?' She stopped, her expression undergoing a sudden change. For a long moment she was silent, brown eyes filled with shame. When she did speak it was on a low, apologetic note. 'Eve, I'm sorry— I shouldn't have said that. I just felt you had to know, that's all. What you do about it is up to you naturally.'

'Thanks.' Eve's smile felt stiff. 'I'll have to think about it.' She got up from the chair, her knees like jelly beneath her. 'I'm going to start packing. We'll need to be on our way after breakfast if we're to give that barbecue you promised!'

She reached her room without seeing anyone, much to her relief. Conversation of any kind was beyond her right now. Her suitcases were stored at the back of the walk-in closet. She dragged them both out and opened them on the bed, taking out the contents of the first drawer her hand happened to reach and starting to fold each item meticulously into place.

Was it true? she wondered blindly. Was Brett really the kind of man who would go behind his father's back to make up to his wife? It didn't seem possible, not from what she knew of him. Yet what *did* she know of him, when it all boiled down? Instinct alone had proved false in many more cases than her own.

The only sure way of learning the truth was by doing as Fleur had suggested and asking him— always providing he was willing to tell her. And if it was the truth, what then? Could she feel the same way about him? She didn't know. Right at this moment she had no feelings at all.

It was dinnertime before she saw him. Seated

across the table from the perceptive blue gaze, she found it difficult to dissemble. Fleur watched them both with sly interest, assuming a bland expression whenever she happened to catch Brett's eye.

The news that the two of them planned on leaving for the Circle Three the next morning elicited little response on Brett's part, plummeting Eve's spirits even further. It could very well be that he intended ending the affair right here and now, although that supposition hardly fitted in with what he had said last night. One thing was certain, the loss of her immediate presence was not going to cut very deep. She might continue to see him, but it would be at his choosing, not hers.

With Alex Shane still a guest in the house, there was no real opportunity to be alone with Brett during the evening. The whole party spent it out on the verandah in the balmy night air, entertained between conversational bouts by the sound of a guitar carrying across from the mobile homes where some kind of function was going on.

'Time we had some kind of affair again ourselves,' said Bart unexpectedly at one point. 'The Diamond Bar barbecues used to be legend in these parts.' He glanced at his son, who lounged in a chair with his feet lifted up to the rail. 'How about it?'

'Sounds a good idea,' came the lazy reply. 'When did you have in mind?'

'Nothing wrong with next weekend, is there? Now that round-up's over folk are ready for a day out. Can you make it down again, Alex?'

'I'll certainly try,' promised the other man. 'It must be nearly three years since . . .' He broke off abruptly in the manner of one about to commit a *faux pas*, shoulders lifting a little uncomfortably. 'Well, a long time anyway.'

Bart finished the sentence for him, his manner unconcerned. 'The last time was just before my accident. Haven't really felt much like socialising since, but it's past time I got started again. The weekend it is. Maria and José will organise everything, the way they always did.'

'Are we invited?' asked Fleur ingenuously, and received an indulgent smile.

'You two are going to be the guests of honour. We'll have every male between sixteen and sixty champing at the bit!'

'Make it twenty-six to thirty,' she retorted smartly, 'and I might be interested!'

That just about let Wade Connors in, Eve reflected dryly. Whether he would be among those invited was another matter—one she doubted Fleur had considered.

Alex smothered a yawn with the back of his hand. 'For what little I've done today, I can't keep my eyes open. Hope nobody minds if I call it a night?'

'I was just thinking along the same lines,' claimed Bart. 'Only don't let it break you three up. It's only just gone half after ten.'

Fleur waited until both men had disappeared indoors before getting slowly and ostentatiously to her feet, her eyes seeking those of her sister with a message in their depths. 'I still have some packing to do. I suppose you'll be around in the morning, Brett?'

'I daresay.' He sounded unconcerned. 'You're not moving a million miles away.'

'Just being polite,' she came back on a note of asperity. 'Thanks for putting up with us!'

The strong mouth tilted. 'No hassle.'

Silence fell heavily between the two of them left

on the verandah once the click of Fleur's high heels had faded into the depth of carpeted floors. Eve gazed straight out across the shadowed homestead to where the fires still flickered between the double row of mobile homes.

'They seem to be having a good time out there,' she commented at length when she could no longer bear the waiting for Brett to speak. 'Is it in aid of anything special?'

'Just a general Saturday night shindig,' he said in the same lazy tone. 'Want to walk over and take a look?'

She hesitated, torn between the need to air her doubts and the desire to leave well alone. 'Won't they mind?' she prevaricated.

'Mind what? Anybody's welcome?' His shrug was more sensed than seen. 'Please yourself, I'm easy either way.'

The decision came without conscious prompting. 'All right, let's.'

Brett came to his feet in one lithe easy movement, dropping down the step and waiting for her to join him. Lit only by the dim verandah lights, his face looked all planes and angles, the blue eyes remote. He made no attempt to touch her as they started across the grass together, stalking at her side like some tall dark shadow in his black shirt and pants.

'You never mentioned that there was a pool at the house,' Eve said after a moment or two. 'Fleur is over the moon!'

'Fleur's an extremist all the way through,' came the dry reply. 'It never occurred to me to mention it. I wasn't trying to sell you the place.'

'No, of course not.' She bit her lip, too well aware that her act was convincing no one. His next words confirmed that notion.

'Suppose you tell me what's on your mind?' he said evenly without breaking stride.

It was too quick and too soon. Instinctively she found herself prevaricating again. 'What makes you think I've anything on my mind?'

'Eyes, ears, and every other damned sense,' he growled softly. I can even scent it.' His glance shifted sideways when she failed to reply, thoughtfully assessing her averted face. 'Going to spit it out, or would you rather I insisted?'

She looked at him then, one swift glance taking in the set of his jaw. 'You sound as if you might already know,' she murmured, still playing for time.

'I might have an idea,' he acknowledged. 'You saw Connors today. There's only one story he could have told you to bring on this kind of reaction.'

Eve shook her head. 'I wasn't the one he told. He took Fleur round the place, and they ... got talking.'

'And she couldn't wait to pass the message on.' His lips twisted. 'It figures.'

Eve waited a full thirty seconds before voicing the question. 'Was Wade lying outright, or simply exaggerating what he saw?'

The dark head didn't turn. 'That would depend on what he says he did see.'

She had been hoping for an outright denial, not this seeming prevarication of his own. A straight answer was the only way of getting to the truth. They weren't touching in any way. Somehow she would have felt better about everything had he taken her hand. She said it abruptly because she wanted to get it over, 'Wade saw you and your stepmother down by the river. He says she was struggling to get away from you.'

The pause before he responded seemed to last

an age. When he did speak it was unemotionally.
'He was right about that—she was.'

Eve stopped in her tracks, fists clenching at her
sides. 'Then it is true! You actually . . .' She broke
off, unable to force the words out from a throat
that ached as badly as hers did at this moment.
She spun round without looking at him. 'I'm going
back to the house!'

He caught her before she had gone three paces,
turning her back to him with a rough hand on her
shoulder. The blue eyes looked almost black in the
cold light of the stars. 'How about listening to my
angle?' he demanded harshly.

'I don't want to know!' The hurt was spreading
through her too fast and fiercely for rationality.
'There's nothing you could say that would excuse
what you did! She was your stepmother—your
father's wife! How could you, Brett?'

It was a long, long moment before he replied to
that, all expression wiped from his face. The hand
fell from her shoulder to be stuck deep into a
trouser pocket. 'You're right. How could I? Run
along, kiddy. You're safer that way.'

Only now did she hesitate, struck by some
underlying note in his voice. 'Brett,' she began, 'I . . .'

'We didn't say goodbye, did we?' he interrupted
with a cynical inflection. 'That's easily remedied.'
Both hands came out of his pockets to seize her in
a grip that hurt, dragging her close up against him.
His lips were cold and hard, pressuring hers back
against her teeth. She tasted blood from the
trapped inner flesh, but had neither strength nor
will to fight back.

He released her so abruptly she almost lost
balance, putting out an involuntary hand for a
support that was as swiftly removed. 'That's for

the last couple of days,' he said. 'Or should I say nights? It's been nice having you.'

Eve stayed frozen to the spot as he turned and moved off in the direction they had been going initially, only now coming to the conclusion that she might have been a little too hasty in her judgment. Brett might have been temporarily carried away by a beautiful and desirable woman, but that didn't necessarily mean he had carried the affair to its natural conclusion. She should have given him the benefit of the doubt and at least listened to what he had to say, she acknowledged painfully.

The temptation to run after him was great. She controlled herself with difficulty. Right now he was angry enough to tell her to go to hell. She had to give him time to simmer down.

She saw no one on the way to her room. In her present state of mind, bed was the last place she wanted to be. Common sense told her to leave the whole thing over until morning at least, only common sense wasn't holding too much sway at the moment. She had to get it over with tonight, she told herself desperately. She had to try to put things right again, even if she failed. How long it would be before Brett returned to the house there was no way of knowing. The only sure way of catching him was by waiting for him in his room—if she dare.

Daring didn't come into it, she decided in the end. She owed him the opportunity to explain. Still fully dressed, she left her room and made her way quietly across to the other wing, locating the correct door and slipping inside with a little prayer of gratitude that doors in this house were never locked. She had only been in the room once before, and that briefly. The decorations were strictly masculine, with lots of wood and leather and a colour scheme of browns and beiges. The bed itself was cut off from the rest of the room by a half wall lined on its far side with wardrobes, the bathroom opening from the rear. Eve found herself an easy chair by a window, not attempting to switch on any lights. The waiting was going to be the hardest part. Brett could well decide to stay out till the early hours if the party over there went on that long.

Despite the state of her mind, Eve dozed off eventually, awakening only when a light clicked on close by where she sat. Brett straightened from the lamp table a few feet away to look at her with sardonically lifted brows.

'Forget something, did we?'

Eve sat up in the chair, putting up an automatic hand to push her hair from her face. His manner was anything but encouraging, but she had to make some attempt.

'I came to say I was sorry for jumping at you so quickly,' she got out.

His expression didn't alter. 'Okay,' he said, 'so you said it. Do you know what time it is?'

'I don't care what time it is.' She was sitting on the extreme edge of the chair, hands gripping the arms. 'Brett, don't make this any more difficult than it is!'

His shrug bespoke total indifference. 'I don't see any difficulty. You made your opinion pretty plain. There's nothing to be said.'

'Yes, there is,' she insisted. 'You asked me to listen to your side of things. That's why I'm here— I want to hear it.'

'Tough.' He hadn't moved, standing there with a look of solid rock about him. 'You had your chance. There isn't going to be another.'

Eve gazed at him helplessly, aware of the implacable set of his jaw. 'I made a mistake,' she said, trying hard not to beg. 'Didn't you ever do something you instantly regretted?'

'More than once,' he admitted. 'This is something else again.'

'Why?'

'Because it involves a part of my life that has nothing whatsoever to do with you in the first place,' he came back hardily. 'So we went to bed a couple of times. Okay, it was pretty good, I wouldn't deny that. Only bedding a woman doesn't give her any kind of rights. That's a small matter most of you overlook. What happened in the past, and what might happen in the future, is my affair and mine only. Clear?'

'It couldn't be more so.' Face white, Eve got to her feet. 'I suppose I should thank you for having me. I'm sure most women would be grateful for the opportunity!'

A muscle twitched suddenly at the side of his jaw. 'Get out of here,' he advised softly, 'before I show you a side of me you wouldn't be grateful for!'

'I'm going, don't worry.' She forced herself to walk forward, refusing to steer a line which would avoid even the narrowest of contacts. 'I'll be out of your hair altogether in the morning. It couldn't have come at a better time.'

Brett made no answer to that. When she closed the door he was still standing where she had left him, back totally unyielding.

CHAPTER EIGHT

THEY took their leave of the Diamond Bar soon after breakfast. Bart was sorry to see them go but willing to rely on Eve's promise to be back. She would have to keep that promise, she knew, regardless of how awkward her visits might prove to be. If Brett had any finer feeling at all, she told herself numbly, he would make certain he was not going to be around when she did come.

Putting on a good face this morning for the benefit of others had taken all she had. She bitterly regretted not having told Wade to come over and pick them when it became obvious that Brett himself would be driving them to their new home. Fleur's move to the rear seat left her with little alternative but to take her own seat at Brett's side, although the very closeness of him made her tremble. It was going to be a long time before she could even think of him without this dreadful ache inside, she acknowledged. Regardless of what he might or might not have done, she still loved him desperately.

He spoke little on the way to the ranch. Fleur did most of the chatting from the back, apparently unaware of any atmosphere between her two companions. Her plans to make for Miami seemed to have been temporarily shelved. Eve wondered if Wade Connors had anything to do with that decision, and whether that would be a good thing or bad. Giving Fleur the details of that story so soon after meeting her was hardly an act to inspire great trust. Yet for all she knew, Fleur herself had been telling the truth when she said she had wormed it out of him. All it would have needed was the slightest hint from Wade to have her hot on the trail, particularly when it concerned a man who had piqued her pride the way Brett had.

What did it matter, anyway? she asked herself wearily. Her own reaction to the story had caused the rift. That Brett had not softened from last night's stance was more than obvious. They were through, and without too much heartache on his part, if appearances were anything to go by. Eve doubted if he would ever know the kind of agony she was going through at this moment. Nothing would ever touch him that deeply.

Wade was waiting for them at the house, along with the two wives he had employed as domestic help. The latter were both women in their forties, one tall and auburn-haired, the other small and dark. They had already been through the whole house gathering dust sheets and vacuuming carpets. The opened windows had vanquished the last trace of that musty smell all empty houses seem to acquire.

Brett refused Fleur's invitation to come indoors for a cup of the coffee Jenny had waiting.

'It isn't all that often I get a chance to see Alex for any length of time,' he said. 'He'll be leaving before dinner.'

'In that case there isn't much point in inviting you to the barbecue we're giving this afternoon,' she reponded sweetly. 'How about yours? Is it still on?'

'If it's what Dad wants it's still on,' he agreed. Just for a moment the blue eyes met Eve's, their expression cool and remote. 'See you.'

'Everything's organised for this afternoon,' Wade told them easily as the sound of the departing jeep faded into the distance. 'The kids can't wait. Laura used to let the older ones use the pool at weekends and vacations. She liked to hear them having a good time, she always said.'

'There's no reason why we shouldn't continue to share it,' said Eve. 'It's more than big enough.'

Wade grinned. 'Mr Cranley's family originated from Texas. Guess he inherited a whole lot more than hard cash.'

'You knew him?' she asked.

He shook his head. 'He was dead before I came to the Circle Three. The previous foreman retired a couple of years back.'

'And you were the next in line?'

'Not exactly.' The inflection was just faintly defensive. 'Laura wanted it that way. She knew I could do the job.'

'Why the inquisition?' demanded Fleur from the far window. 'You're going to need a foreman, you know.'

'Yes, I do know.' Eve smiled at the man in front of her. 'I didn't mean to sound as if I were quizzing you. We'll still be running the ranch at a loss, of course.'

'But you will be running it. It's what Laura would have wanted.' He ran his fingers along the rim of the hat he held in his hands, gaze steady. 'You can trust me. I never let Laura down.'

'I'm sure you didn't.' Eve was speaking the truth. She did trust him; that was what made everything so much harder to bear.

The barbecue was a howling success. Eve enjoyed it herself. Looking round at one point at these people who were now her and Fleur's employees, she vowed there and then that the Circle Three would continue so long as her income would cover it, no matter what pressures were brought to bear on her to sell out. Because the fight was on again, there was nothing surer. Brett would stop at nothing to get his hands on the land he already considered a part of his own.

There was a whole lot that was new to learn, and Eve was impatient to do so. She spent the first couple of days going over the whole routine of running a ranch with Wade, until Fleur expressed her dissatisfaction with that particular arrangement.

'Don't think you're going to steal Wade the way you stole Brett,' she warned the third morning at breakfast, 'because it won't work.' She waited a moment. 'Eve, are you listening to me?'

'What?' Eve lifted her eyes from the ledger she was studying, eyeing her sister with questioning expression. 'Sorry, I wasn't listening.'

Fleur breathed hard through her nose. 'That's obvious. I said keep your hands off Wade, to put it as plainly as possible.'

'Wade?' Eve was confused. 'What are you talking about?'

'You know very well what I'm talking about. You might have seen him first, but I'm the one he's interested in. And not just for what Brett saw in you either!'

Eve took a moment to gather herself before answering that, too well aware that Fleur was already regretting the statement. 'I'm sure you're right. He's always bringing your name up on one pretext or another.'

Her sister's colour had risen. 'That was a rotten

crack,' she admitted. 'I don't know what gets into me sometimes.'

'It doesn't matter,' Eve said softly.

'Yes, it does. We've always been good friends. I'd hate not to be any more.' Fleur paused, her expression frankly curious. 'What exactly happened between you and Brett? Did he deny it?'

Eve felt her throat close up the way it always did when Brett's name was mentioned. 'It isn't important,' she said. 'I made a mistake getting too close too soon, that's all. I'll put it down to experience and benefit from it.'

'Sez you!' The snort was derisive. 'Eve, I'm not that thick. He really hurt you, didn't he?'

There was little use in pretending. She lifted her shoulders. 'All right, so he really hurt me. That isn't to say I didn't ask for it.' She finished her coffee in a gulp, pushing back her chair as she did so. 'I'm off. We're fetching in Aunt Laura's mare this morning. Why don't you come instead of lazing around the pool?' Her smile was deliberatively provocative. 'That way you'd be able to keep an eye on the man yourself.'

Fleur laughed. 'I might even get him to teach me to ride!'

'Not the mare,' Eve said swiftly. 'I'd like to keep her for my own use, if you don't mind.'

'One horse is as good as another to a blind man,' came the blithe misquote. 'Just so long as you appreciate who Wade belongs to.'

'I think Wade is man enough to decide that for himself,' Eve replied. 'But if it's of any interest, he isn't my type.'

And in another couple of weeks he probably wouldn't be Fleur's either, she reflected with irony, going out of the door. The latter had little staying power when it came to singleness of heart.

The chestnut mare was out to pasture with several other of the ranch horses at present, but unlike the others she had not been brought in over the past few months, finding her shelter from the elements in a lean-to shed occupying a corner of the field.

'She hasn't been ridden for over a year,' Wade warned as he opened the gate to take his own mount through while the two girls watched from the near fence. 'I'll get a rope on her and we'll see, but if she's gone wild she's going to be no use to you till she's been broken again.'

'If she's gone wild I shan't want her broken again,' Eve came back. 'We'll just leave her right here where she's happy.' She met the glance turned back on her and grinned up at him. 'Blame my nationality—we're a sentimental lot when it comes to animals!'

'Not all of us,' claimed Fleur. She took off her hat and waved it in the air. 'Go to it, cowboy!'

Wade went to it, singling out the animal he wanted from the rest with a skill and expertise Eve recognised from past experience. The mare reared as the rope settled about her neck, whinnying frantically and pulling against the unaccustomed restriction. She was a beautiful animal, standing about fifteen hands, her mane and tail tossing in the breeze. Wade brought her across, dismounting to fasten the rope end close up to the fence post.

'She's not going to like that saddle across her back again,' he said, studying the heaving, sweat-glistened flanks. 'Laura only rode her for a few months from breaking. If you'd been a regular rider . . .'

'I'd like to try,' Eve said stubbornly. 'Let me talk to her before you do anything else.'

The foreman gave in with a shrug. 'It's your neck. Laura called her Caprice—bit fancy for a horse, I always thought, but being English yourself, guess you'll like it.'

Eve did like it. She took her time approaching the animal, seeing the ears flick towards her as she murmured the name. There was a momentary shying away as her hand touched the smooth neck, then the mare stood still, trembling a little but suffering the soothing, stroking motion without protest. Still talking to her, Eve moved the hand up and over to pat the white blaze down the front of her face, breathing down her nose so that the animal could get her scent, the way a certain British trainer would have advocated! Caprice dropped her head and nuzzled the fingers held to her mouth, whickering softly.

'Well, I'll be damned!' said Wade. 'You must have more of Laura in you than I thought!' He moved to seize the saddle he had thrown over the fence. 'Let's try this.'

The mare sidestepped nervously when he threw the leathers across her back. Eve stopped him from continuing and took over herself, reaching under the taut belly for the girth without thinking of the possible consequences should the mare object. But she didn't object. She allowed the girths to be buckled without moving a muscle, simply rolling her eyes backwards as if trying to see what was going on. The bridle was next. Eve held her breath as she slid the bit into line with that mouth full of teeth, but it opened automatically to receive it, the great tongue rolling the metal in a comfortable position.

'You're not going right up?' asked Wade on a surprised note as Eve gathered both reins and moved back to lift a foot to the stirrup.

'Nothing ventured, nothing gained,' she quipped over a shoulder, refusing to allow herself to be deterred. 'If I weren't fresh out from England you wouldn't even think about it.'

'Guess there might be something in that,' he agreed dryly. 'Okay, so let me give you a boost.'

There was no movement from the mare as he hoisted her upwards. Eve took care to settle herself gently down into the saddle, leaning forward to rub the hard knob of bone between the pricked ears. 'Untie the rope,' she said.

Wade did so, standing back to watch critically as she turned the animal's head out from the fence and urged her into a walk. The gait was so comfortable she immediately felt secure, prompting first a gentle trot and then a slow canter in an ever-widening circle until she finally came to a halt opposite where the other two waited.

'She's fine,' she called exultantly. 'We're both fine! Open the gate, will you, Wade—I'm going to ride her out for a while.'

'Running before you've learned to walk,' he mocked, but he no longer looked concerned. 'Bring her in when you're through and I'll have Sam check her shoes.'

Eve lifted a hand to Fleur as she passed through the gateway, heading down the track by which they had come. There was a fork some few hundred yards along beyond a clump of trees. She chose the left simply because the jeep would be taking the right, feeling her spirits soar as the mare responded to her guidance. For what amounted to her fifth time on horseback she wasn't doing at all badly. Some people could achieve instant rapport with animals. Perhaps she was one of them without even having realised it before.

The track she was following eventually joined up with a wider though still unmetalled road. From here she could see a couple of the taller buildings in Leesville on the far horizon. Why not ride into town and buy herself a pair of those cowboy boots she had seen last week? she thought. She was certainly going to need them if she intended riding regularly.

'And we are, aren't we, girl?' she said to her mount, patting the glossy neck. 'This is going to be the start of a fine relationship!'

It took her little more than twenty minutes to complete the journey into town. Riding down the main street, Eve felt totally at home. It was difficult to believe that she had only been in the country a matter of days. The old life had retreated to a place far distant in her memory.

An old hitching rail still stood in the side street close by the store where she had seen the boots. She left Caprice standing quite contentedly while she went to buy. Finding a pair to fit her size five feet was no problem, choosing the tooled pattern in the leather something else again. Eventually she plumped for a pair in a shade of beige which toned with her hat, paying by credit card and electing to keep them on. Her shoes were packed into a neat parcel she could fasten on to the back of her saddle with the string provided.

There was a jeep parked at the end of the little alley. Brett sat behind the wheel, his hat tipped to the back of his head in a manner familiar enough to start the heartache even before she reached him.

'I recognised the mare,' he said without

preamble as she came level with the vehicle. 'Not exactly a beginner's mount, I'd have said.'

'She's as quiet as a lamb,' Eve defended shortly.

'Sometimes. She used to be pretty unpredictable—that's what Laura liked about her.'

'She's a year older,' Eve pointed out. 'Maybe, like all of us, she's learned wisdom.'

His lips twisted suddenly. 'Maybe you're right. It's never too late. Going straight back, are you?'

'Yes.' She couldn't bear another moment of this stilted conversation. 'Tell your father I'll be over tomorrow to see him.'

'Why not phone him and tell him yourself!' he suggested. 'He's been waiting for you to get in touch.' He paused. 'Incidentally, the barbecue is definitely on—I left a message at the house earlier. I hope you're planning on coming.'

For his father's sake, Eve reminded herself painfully, not for his own. 'Of course,' she said. 'I wouldn't miss it. Goodbye, Brett.'

'Nice meeting you.' The tone was sardonic. 'Just watch yourself with that animal.'

'I can cope, thanks.' She made no attempt to keep the sharpness from her voice. 'One thing I don't need is your advice!'

His shrug was indifferent. 'Suit yourself. See you at the weekend.'

Eve heard him drive away as she walked towards the mare. She swallowed on the hard lump in her throat. Some day it would stop hurting like this. Some day she would be able to look back and smile at the memory.

She was some couple of miles out of town when she caught the sound of a car coming up in her wake. Without turning to look round, she knew it was Brett. What she wasn't certain of was whether he had deliberately followed her or, having completed his own business in town, was simply on his way back to the Diamond Bar. The turn-off was another mile or so ahead. On impulse, she put Caprice into a canter, using the grass verge in order to provide softer passage and urging her on to greater efforts as the jeep drew level.

'Cut it out, you crazy little fool!' yelled Brett, keeping pace. 'Pull her up!'

'Any time *I* want to,' Eve yelled back. 'Watch out for yourself!'

His reply was under his breath, but from the set of his lips it was vicious. He pulled ahead, his foot hard on the accelerator. Eve waited until he was several hundred yards on before starting to rein the mare in, her heart missing a beat when the animal refused to respond. The canter had stretched to a full gallop, smooth while the ground beneath the flying hooves remained unbroken, but needing only the slightest of stumbles to have her unseated. She leaned back on the reins with all her strength, knowing even as she did so that she didn't have enough weight to stop a horse with the bit between its teeth. The fact that it was her own fault was totally beside the point. She had no idea what to do except hang on like grim death and hope the animal beneath her would eventually run out of steam.

There was open country at the roadside. Caprice veered to the left without any direction on Eve's part, thundering across the grass like a streak of greased lightning. Vaguely, Eve was aware of sounds behind her, but she daren't turn her head to look for fear of falling off. When the jeep hove into view on the periphery of her vision she could scarcely believe it.

Slowly, with the vehicle bouncing madly under him, Brett drew ahead, inclining inwards to head the mare off her chosen path until she was literally running in a circle. The strain was beginning to tell, the pace gradually dropping. Eve's attempts to regain control eventually bore fruit, but by the time she did manage to pull the animal to a complete halt her palms were rubbed raw by the leather.

Brett was out of the jeep almost before it had stopped, yanking her roughly down out of the saddle.

'You could have been killed!' he gritted. 'You damned little idiot, you might have broken your neck!'

Her senses still spinning, her hands hurting like fire, Eve could take no more. 'Go to hell!' she spat at him. 'It's my neck!'

There was a moment when he was totally still, only the glitter in his eyes betraying his reaction. A stand of trees hid them from the distant road. So far as the eye could see, they were entirely alone. She fought as he pushed her down into the grass, clawing at his face with frenzied fingers only to have her wrists seized in a grip of steel. It was like that first time by the river, only this time he wasn't going to be stopped by a few taunts. His mouth was savage on hers.

And then suddenly it didn't matter any more. Nothing mattered any more except the need coursing through her. She softened beneath him, arms sliding about his neck, lips answering the hard demand. His hand was inside her shirt, curving to the shape of her, his finger and thumb testing the firm-peaked flesh with a touch that dragged a moan from deep down inside her. She could feel his hardness pressing into her and she wanted more—wanted it all. She breathed his name against his lips.

It was Brett who called a halt, rolling away from her with a smothered exclamation to lie on his back with an arm up shielding his eyes from the sun.

'Not this time, honey,' he grated. 'We've been down that path before!'

Eve lay still, trying to get a hold on herself. She felt shamed, only too conscious of her own weakness. There was to be no making up; he had made that clear. He would even deny himself something he obviously still wanted in order to prove it to her.

Caprice was peacefully cropping grass a few yards away. With an effort, Eve pushed herself upright and then to her feet, crossing to gather the mare's reins.

'You're not thinking of getting on her again?' asked Brett, coming to a sitting position.

She answered without turning her head. 'Wasn't it you who said if you fell off a horse you'd get straight back on again?'

'Providing I knew what I was doing. You know as much about horses as I do about piano playing!' He was on his feet now, dusting himself down with a hard hand. 'I'll tie her behind the car and take you both home.'

'No!' The denial was fierce. 'I'll walk her home if necessary, but I won't have you telling me what to do!'

'I wouldn't trust you to have the sense to stay out of the saddle,' he retorted harshly. 'Either you get in the jeep or I'll put you in. It's your choice.'

He would do it, she knew. Pride choking her, she went over and slid into the passenger seat. The keys were still in the ignition. For a blind moment she was tempted to move across and take off without him, but only for a moment. They had been that way before too, and much good it had done her in the long run. Better by far to let him have his way.

They drove back to the Circle Three slowly in order not to put too much strain on the animal fastened behind. Wade was coming out of one of the barns as they drew up in the yard.

'What happened?' he demanded.

'What you might have expected to happen with a novice rider and a temperamental animal,' said Brett caustically. 'If she'd been injured you'd have been directly to blame.'

'That isn't fair!' Eve burst out, seeing Wade's face tense. 'If you must know, he tried to dissuade me from riding her.'

'Then you're an even bigger idiot than I thought,' came the clipped reply. 'Try using a little of that famed British sense next time.'

Wade unfastened the mare from the rear of the jeep, holding her still as the vehicle moved off. The eyes resting on Eve's face were sympathetic.

'Doesn't give much quarter, does he? Never did. What really happened?'

'She ran away with me,' Eve admitted. 'I couldn't hold her. Brett came after us in the jeep and headed her off.'

'Pity,' he said, stroking the soft nose. 'I guess that finishes it.'

'If you mean shall I be riding her again, the answer is yes,' she came back resolutely. 'Only next time I'll be prepared.'

His glance was admiring. 'I'll say one thing for you, you've got guts!'

'Thanks.' Right now she needed all the approbation she could find. 'Where's Fleur?'

'Out at the pool. I guess.' The look in his eyes changed character. 'A regular water baby, that sister of yours. Think she's going to stay around long?'

Eve lifted a pair of deliberately casual shoulders. 'As long as she feels she wants to. Even then, it will still be home.'

'You mean she isn't planning on going back to England?'

'I'd say that was the last place she'd think of going for quite some time.'

Wade was obviously smitten, she reflected wryly, going on into the house as the foreman led Caprice away. She only hoped Fleur would let him down lightly when the time came.

The telephone drew her eye. Brett wouldn't be home for at least another ten minutes—if that was where he was heading. Now, if any, was the time to call his father.

Bart answered personally from the study where he was, he said, going through some papers. He sounded a little strained. Eve hesitated to ask if anything was wrong.

'I hear the barbecue is all fixed,' she said on a bright note. 'I saw Brett in town a while ago.'

'All fixed,' Bart confirmed. There was a pause before he added, 'Don't I get to see you before then?'

'I could ride over in the morning,' she said, knowing Brett was unlikely to be around the house before lunch. 'You could give me coffee.'

'Anything you like.' The strain was still there, but muted. 'I've missed you, Eve. The place seems empty.'

With just the two of them in a house the size of that one it *was* empty, she thought in sympathy. Maria and José kept themselves very much to themselves; certainly they were neither of them great conversationalists. Bart loved to talk, about anything and everything. Over these past three years since his accident he had found some consolation in books, his tastes wide and varied. He had ploughed the whole way through *War and Peace*, although admitting to finding great chunks of it dull reading. Eve supposed it was that same perseverence which had enabled him to come to terms with his disability in the end, uphill though the struggle must have been. She had a lot of time for Bart Hanson. It was his son who made the relationship so difficult, and that wasn't going to change. Not now.

CHAPTER NINE

THE mare looked thoroughly docile when Wade brought her up to the house the following morning, her coat gleaming like silk in the bright sunlight.

'I think you're mad to trust that animal again,' said Fleur bluntly, having heard the bare bones of yesterday's episode. 'Next time Brett may not be around to save your skin!'

'There won't be a next time,' Eve returned firmly, accepting Wade's hoist into the saddle and gathering the reins. 'Forewarned is forearmed.'

'And over-confidence goeth before a fall,' came the smart retort. 'Yes, I know it should be pride. With you it's more or less the same thing.'

That statement was a little too close to the truth for comfort. Eve chose to turn a deaf ear. 'See you later,' she said, bringing the mare's head round with a steady hand. 'I'll be back for lunch.'

The ride over to the Diamond Bar proved uneventful. Having put the mare through her paces with perfect accord, Eve came to the conclusion that she had probably been spooked by the sound of the jeep so close behind her. Brett should have had more sense than to come up so fast, she told herself in self-righteous mitigation. He might have saved her neck, but he had been the one to put it at risk in the first place.

Bart was waiting for her out on the verandah. One of the hands came and took Caprice from her to turn her loose in the corral until needed again.

'So yesterday's fright didn't put you off any?' Bart observed mildly when she was seated alongside him with a cup of coffee in front of her. 'Brett was right about that.'

Eve kept her expression strictly controlled. 'What did he tell you?'

'He said the mare ran away from you.' He studied her for a moment, eyes shrewd. 'Was there more?'

Her shrug made light of the question. 'It sums it up. I had no trouble with her this morning.'

'So I gathered. The two of you look made for each other.' He smiled reminiscently. 'Seeing you coming through those gates just now I'd have sworn it was Laura. She turned me down, you know.'

Eve looked at him in sudden realisation. 'No, I didn't know. When . . .'

'I asked her to marry me the year after Jos died,' he said levelly. 'I didn't expect to take his place—it just seemed right, that's all. There we were, two lonely people who got along real good. Only Laura couldn't see the sense in it. She said she'd have felt disloyal to Jos's memory.'

'I'm sorry.' Eve said it with sincerity, sensing a deeper disappointment than he appeared to be acknowledging. 'I suppose she didn't feel able to go back on her promise to keep the Circle Three going as a separate concern.'

'She could have done that too. Brett's the one who's interested in incorporating that land.' The smile was faint. 'Comes of having a tidy mind, I guess. The Circle Three's been a thorn in his side for years, especially as Jos was running the place at a loss. You realise he hasn't given up on it yet?'

Eve nodded, not quite meeting the older eyes. 'I realise. I can be stubborn too.'

'I guessed that the first day we met,' he came back on a dry note. 'Thought you'd managed to straighten out some of your differences, though. Seems I was wrong.'

This time she had to look at him, her expression wry. 'Your son isn't an easy man to stay on the right side of, Mr Hanson.'

'Bart,' he said. 'Make it Bart.' It was his turn to shrug. 'I warned you he was strong-willed. I'd have said if anybody could handle him you could.'

She tried to keep her tone light. 'It just goes to show how deceptive appearances can be.'

'Doesn't it just?' He shook his head. 'I'm not going to ask what happened between you two. I just had hopes, that's all.'

'I've barely been here a week,' she protested softly. 'Even if . . .'

'Like I said, I thought you could handle him. It's time he thought about taking a wife. I want to know there's going to be a grandson to carry things on before I go.'

'You're too young to be talking about going anywhere,' she retorted swiftly. 'There's plenty of time. He's only thirty-two himself.'

Bart snorted. 'I was twenty-five when I got hitched, twenty-six when he was born. I wanted a whole passel of kids, only his mother wasn't able to have any more after him.'

'You blamed her for that?'

'Hell no! What do you take me for? She was a lovely woman all the way through.'

'Sorry,' she murmured. 'I misunderstood.'

'Half the world's problems are caused that way,' he said, but there was no real censure in his voice.

'I've made my share of mistakes. Diane was only one of them.'

Eve hesitated before voicing the question. 'How did you meet her?'

The smile was grim. 'She was a friend of a friend doing a tour of the Southern states. She came to stay a week, we were married within the month. There's . . .'

'I know,' Eve interceded smoothly, 'there's no fool like an old fool! Except that you aren't old now, so you certainly weren't then. If she left you simply because of the accident then she wasn't worth a great deal anyway.'

'My son's words exactly.' He looked down at his empty cup, his mouth pulled into an equally empty smile. 'He never approved of the marriage. He thought she was out for what she could get. Seems he might have been right. I've been keeping her in pretty comfortable circumstances this past three years, now she's decided she wants a divorce with appropriate settlement—in her case, a couple of million dollars.'

Eve blinked. 'Can she claim that much?'

'With a clever lawyer, maybe. Oh, I can afford it. What hurts is the timing. Yesterday would have been our fourth anniversary; the papers came in the morning post.'

Bitch! thought Eve. Yet knowing that provided no excuse for Brett. Whatever her faults, Diane had rejected his advances—according to Wade's version, at least. Could the latter possibly have been mistaken in what he had seen? It hardly seemed likely. Diane had been struggling to get away. Why else would she do that unless Brett's attentions had been unwelcome?

'What are you going to do?' she asked.

The greying head turned slowly from side to side. 'I don't know. Brett would want me to fight it.'

'It isn't his life.'

'He won't see it that way.' His head lifted suddenly. 'He's here now.'

Eve looked out across the yard, her heart missing a beat when she saw the jeep heading towards the house. She had counted on Brett not coming in before lunch, if then. He was the last person she wanted to see. Not quite true, she corrected herself ruefully. He was the last person she could face with any equilibrium.

'I should be going,' she said, stirring herself to action. 'I told Fleur I'd be back before lunch.'

'It's barely gone eleven,' Bart pointed out. 'Look, I said I didn't want to know what had happened between you two, and I meant it, only don't run out on me now. I need some support.'

'Against your own son?' she chided.

'Against my own son,' he agreed. 'I want to settle this out of court without having to see her again. He'll be on a plane to L.A. first thing in the morning, if I know him. You could add weight to the argument.'

Eve wanted to laugh. A fat lot of good her opinion would do! Nevertheless, she subsided back into her seat. 'I'll try,' she promised.

Brett brought the jeep right to the step, coming on up to where they sat, expression fixed.

'Still ignoring advice?' he observed, leaning his length against the rail. 'Connors could find you another animal without looking too far.'

'Except that I prefer this one,' Eve returned coolly. 'Predictability can be *awfully* boring.' She deliberately emphasised her accent, watching his lip curl with a bland little smile of her own. 'I don't get caught the same way twice.'

'Confidence being the keynote,' put in Bart lightly before his son could answer. 'Have you finished for the day, or is this just a passing visit?'

'I'm all through,' Brett acknowledged. 'Thought you might like a trip into town for lunch. It's been over a month since you left the ranch.'

There was a moment when Bart appeared to be about to turn the offer down, then apparently he changed his mind. 'Sounds good,' he agreed. 'Eve, why don't you come too?'

She shook her head, avoiding Brett's eyes. 'It's a nice idea, but I told Fleur I'd be back for lunch.'

'Call her,' Brett suggested unexpectedly. 'She's not a kid. She can feed herself.' He registered the jerk of her head with sardonic expression. 'You wouldn't turn my father down, would you?'

'It's her own choice,' responded the latter. 'Don't pressure the girl!'

Eve came to a swift decision, her smile for Bart and Bart only. 'I'd like to come, very much. Caprice will be safe enough in the corral till we get back, I expect?'

'As houses.' Brett straightened his body. 'I need a shower and a clean shirt. Shan't keep you long.'

'Thanks for not opting out,' said Bart softly as his son disppeared indoors. 'I'd like to get away from the house for a spell.' He rolled his chair out from the table. 'Why don't you go and call Fleur while I get myself organised!'

There was a telephone in an alcove close by the outer doors. Eve took the chair beside it and dialled the Circle Three number, conscious of the tremor in her fingers as she did so. She only had to close her eyes to see the tanned, naked body standing beneath the jet of water, to remember the moments they had shared. Loving Brett was a disease it was going to take a long time to clear from her system. She could pretend to others, but not to herself.

Fleur received the news with a surprising lack of objection. Yet why so surprising? Eve asked herself after she had finished the call. Brett was right about that much: Fleur was no child to be looked after and indulged. She had her own life to lead, and fully intended doing so. She herself must be prepared to do the same.

Brett came through while she was still sitting there thinking about it, glancing at her with lifted brows.

'Okay?'

'Fine,' she said hastily, gathering herself together. 'Your father isn't ready to go yet.'

'No rush. I have to swap transport anyway—this one isn't geared to take the chair.'

He went outside. A moment later Eve heard the jeep move off. Only then did she follow, waiting at the rail as she had waited that first morning. Eight days ago, that was all. It scarcely seemed possible. So much had changed since then, and not for the better.

The second vehicle looked very little different from the first until the electric platform was extended and lowered. Secured by a couple of clamps, the wheelchair was lifted into position at the driver's side in one smooth operation, leaving Eve to take a rear seat.

'I had a runabout converted in similar fashion to drive myself,' Bart acknowledged when she commented admiringly on the idea. 'Don't use it much. Not many places inside my comfort limits.'

'There's the Circle Three,' Eve pointed out. 'We'd

love to see you over there. It would make a change, if nothing else.'

'Worth thinking about,' he agreed as Brett got behind the wheel and started the engine. 'I might just take you up on that.'

Leesville's main street was thronged with people, the store doing good business.

'It's market day,' Bart explained, lifting a hand in answer to yet another familiar greeting from the sidewalk as the jeep progressed. 'We're going to be lucky to find any room at the General.'

'General?' asked Eve curiously.

'The local inn. Used to be called Charlie's Place till Bob took over. Full name Robert E. Leeway. Memories stay alive round these parts.'

'I told Bob to save a table,' Brett interceded. 'They can always lay another place.'

His father grinned. 'Real sure I'd be coming, weren't you!'

'Real sure I was going to work pretty hard at persuading you,' came the calm agreement. 'Guess all it needed was the right approach.' He drew the jeep to a halt outside a yellow brick building that was a far cry from Eve's idea of a public house. 'Just stay put till I get round there, will you. That lever's sticking.'

Eve slid out the driving side of the vehicle, following him round to stand on the sidewalk watching him handle the chair lift.

'Glad to see you getting out some, Bart!' exclaimed one hearty-looking woman in passing. 'Can't stop now—things to do. See you Saturday.'

'Bank manager's wife,' said Bart for Eve's benefit as they moved on into the General. 'Mary Pierce by name. Harry, you've already met.'

'How many are coming on Saturday?' she asked, and saw the strong shoulders lift.

'It's going to be open house. All I had to do was start the ball rolling with a few calls.' He held out his hand to the burly man who seemed to be standing guard over the dim, cool lobby area. 'Hear you have a table for us, Bob. We brought an extra.'

'No hassle. Good to see you.' The smile turned in Eve's direction was easy. 'What do you think to our little town?'

'I come from a small town myself,' she acknowledged, smiling back. 'It isn't so different.'

'Then you'll not be running off to Miami every five minutes looking for excitement?'

'Wild horses wouldn't drag me away from the Circle Three,' she responded with deliberation. 'I'm here to stay.'

The nod was approving. 'That's the kind of spirit we need round here! I've put you up at the top near the window, Brett. Maybe you'd like to go on in while I get one of the boys to come and lay another place.'

The restaurant was also cool and dim, every table but one already taken. Their progression across the room brought familiar comment from every quarter. Introduced a dozen times, Eve was thankful to sit down at last, although total relaxation was out of the question with Brett sitting right opposite where he could see every nuance of expression in her face.

The food was good without being in any way pretentious. For her main course, Eve chose to visit the superb American-style salad bar stretching almost the full length of the room, filling a plate from the various dishes and topping the whole lot with a dollop of blue cheese.

'I'd feel downright greedy if I didn't happen to know the total calorie count was less than two hundred,' she laughed on returning to the table where the two men were tackling huge steaks with all the trimmings.

'You don't need to figure-watch,' stated Bart with derision. 'You're built how a woman should be built—leastways, nobody would ever take you for a boy—eh Brett?'

'No way,' agreed the latter without taking his eyes from Eve's. There was a cynicism in the blue depths. 'Single-figure hips and a flat chest never did a thing for me.'

No doubt Diane had been a fine figure of a woman too, reflected Eve with a cynicism of her own, forcing herself to hold his gaze. She knew Bart was watching the two of them, and wondered what he was thinking. High hopes, he had said earlier. Well, no higher than hers had been. There might once have been a chance, but she had put paid to that. If she could turn back the clock she might well handle the whole situation in a different fashion.

Bart waited until they were having coffee before bringing up the subject of the divorce. Brett's reaction was immediate and explosive.

'The hell with settling out of court! She's had enough out of you this past three years to set her up for life!'

'A final settlement would get her off my back,' his father responded mildly. 'Okay, maybe she's pushing it a bit high, but there has to be a starting point for negotiations. Alex would take care of it.'

The blue eyes were like chips of steel. '*I* could take care of it.'

'How?'

'My own way.'

Bart smiled a little and shrugged. 'Threats aren't going to work. She's on pretty firm ground and she knows it.'

Brett wasn't giving an inch. 'After the way she walked out on you she'll be short on sympathy.'

'Doubt it. A young and beautiful woman tied to a helpless old cripple—how could she be expected to take it?' The tone was dry. 'Could you do it, Eve?'

The pause stretched. Eve sensed the narrowing of Brett's gaze as the seconds ticked by, yet couldn't bring herself to look at him. 'It would depend on how deeply my feelings were involved,' she said at last. 'If I cared so little for someone that the question of going or staying even arose then there wouldn't be any point in pretending.'

It was Brett who spoke first. 'Maybe I was wrong on that sympathy angle.'

'You're putting words in my mouth,' she retorted, keeping both voice and tone under control. 'I was asked a straight question.'

'And you gave an honest answer.' Bart shook his head at his son. 'I brought her into it.'

'Okay,' came the laconic response, 'so let's hear the rest of it.' He was addressing Eve, lips thinned. 'Do you think he should settle out of court?'

She took a long, slow breath, seeing the taut stretch of tanned skin over facial muscle, the chill in his eyes. 'I think you should let your father make up his own mind,' she said steadily. 'He's the only one who knows what peace of mind is worth to him.'

There was no alteration of expression, just a hardening of the ice. 'I guess that says it all. Did you want any more coffee?'

Eve shook her head. She wanted badly to retract, to wipe that look from his face, but Bart had first claim on her support. Brett was too accustomed to his own way, too sure of his own

judgment. Loving a man didn't have to blind one
to his faults.

By common if unspoken consent, the whole
subject was shelved on the journey back to the
Diamond Bar. Bart kept the conversation going
with a lightness of touch Eve found admirable in
the circumstances. What would happen where
Diane was concerned she had no way of knowing,
and no intention of asking. If Brett stuck to his
implied word, the decision was in his father's
court.

It was only now that she allowed herself to
wonder if her declaration had been as purely
objective as she had imagined. If she were to be
totally honest with herself she had to doubt it.
Brett's handling of the situation would have meant
a personal meeting with the woman, with who
knew what results? I was saving him from himself,
she thought with irony. *My* interests don't even
come into it!

It was gone two-thirty by the time they reached
the house. Eve refused Bart's invitation to come
in, saying she had to get back.

'Stay put,' Brett advised briefly. 'I'll run you
across to the corral.'

She could have walked, but there was no point
in arguing the toss. He saw the chair safely up the
ramp on to the verandah, then came back to get
behind the wheel again without bothering to
glance her way. Bart lifted a hand in farewell as
they moved off.

There was only one animal in the small corral
behind one of the barns. Eve viewed the lovely
Palomino gelding with an appreciative eye,
admiring the combination of golden coat and
flowing cream mane and tail.

'He's beautiful!' she said. 'What's his name?'

'Misty,' Brett replied. There was a momentary pause before he added smoothly, 'He's yours in exchange for the mare.'

'No!' She swung round from the high fence, standing with her back pressed against the bars and anger in her eyes. 'You're not doing that with me!'

'I've done it.' He was totally unmoved. 'I gave orders to have her taken away when I came to get the car before we left. He's a good fast mover, and he's reliable. He won't break your neck.'

'It wasn't the mare who killed my aunt,' she responded bitterly.

'Only because Laura was a brilliant horse-woman. She had problems with the animal more than once.' He paused again, expression unrelenting. 'Do you know what *loco* means?'

Eve hesitated, torn between conflicting emotions. 'Short for locomotive?' she suggested on a flippant note which sounded false even to her own ears.

Brett curled a lip. 'It's no joking matter. The dam should never have been bred. She came close to trampling one of the Circle Three boys to death one time for no reason at all. It's in the bloodline.'

'Caprice is *not* dangerous.' Eve's tone was low, the tremor barely concealed.

'Only when something sparks her off,' he returned on the same hard note. 'And that will be more frequently the older she gets. That's the pattern it follows.'

'I don't believe it!' She came away from the fence, body taut as a bowstring. 'Where is she? In the barn?'

She was moving as she spoke, veering towards the closed doors. There was a small personal entrance set within the larger frames. Blind anger drove her on through it. A shaft of sunlight from the open loading hatch at loft level revealed a row of stalls to one side of the building. Three horses were in occupation, but none of them was the one she sought. Turning from her inspection of the final and empty stall, she found Brett leaning a hand against a nearby post.

'Satisfied?' he asked.

'No!' The fury had mounted to ungovernable proportions. 'The penalty for horse stealing used to be hanging. I wonder what the county sheriff will make of it now!'

'You'll have your chance to find out,' he said. 'Want to call him from the house?'

The fire went out of her suddenly, leaving her gazing at him with darkened, almost pleading eyes. 'Brett, don't treat me like a child. You don't have any right to do this, and you know it!'

'I have the right to be concerned for your neck,' he came back roughly. 'If you weren't so damned mule-headed you'd know I was making sense. Why take a risk just to prove something to me?'

She bit her lip, recognising the truth when she heard it. One hand went up to nervously smooth her hair, the other seeking a stall post for her support. 'It's your way of going about things,' she said at length. 'You walk all over people. If you'd told me about the inheritance factor first . . .'

'It wouldn't have made any difference.' The tone was flat. 'You go by your instincts, don't you? Well, this time I went by mine.'

She said painfully, 'If you're talking about the other night, I'm prepared to listen to your angle now.'

'Except that I'm not prepared to put it.' His face

was in shadow, his eyes impossible to read. There was a pause before he added evenly, 'You can take it or leave it on that basis.'

'I don't think I under ...' she began, and stopped at the impatient shake of his head.

'You understand. If we get together again it's on those terms.'

Eve was very still, unable to tear her eyes away from the tall, lean figure. She could feel her heart thudding against her rib cage, her every instinct urging her to give in and go to him. Diane was in the past. No matter what had happened between them, perhaps she should be allowed to stay there.

'Do you want to?' she asked thickly. 'Get together again, I mean?'

'I wouldn't be standing here talking about it if I didn't,' he said. 'Neither would you.' He studied her without moving. 'It's your choice.'

'Yes.' The single word dropped from her lips almost of its own volition. She saw him straighten, felt the quivering start deep as he came purposefully towards her. 'Someone might come!'

'Nobody's going to come,' he said. 'They're all employed elsewhere. There's just the two of us, Eve. We have a lot of catching up to do.'

She went into his arms without further protest, hungrily meeting his lips. Passion flared swiftly between them, mounting to fever pitch as he tugged her shirt free of her waistband and ran his hands over warm, bare flesh,. She felt herself lifted and carried further into the stall, felt the prickle of straw through her clothing when he laid her down in the loosely piled stack at the rear.

The smell of dried hay mingled with the pungent warmth of animal flesh in her nostrils, stirring her most primitive senses. In shedding her clothing she also shed every last vestige of restriction: she ran her hands over the fine, strong body, urging him on to surge after powerful surge until they could neither of them hold out any longer against the flooding tide.

'It's been too long,' Brett murmured close by her ear some unknown time later. 'I never knew anyone quite like you, Eve.'

Not even Diane? she wanted to ask, but she knew better. Strength of mind was one quality Brett wasn't short of. If she broke their agreement he would drop her like a hot potato, no matter what it cost him in regrets.

'We should get dressed,' she said softly, not really wanting to move at all. 'I'd hate to get caught in this state!'

'The way nature intended?' He was smiling, his head lifted so he could see her face. 'There's time yet. Just stay the way you are.' His eyes travelled downwards over her body, pale-skinned in the dim light penetrating to this part of the barn, fingertips lightly following the same path. 'Smooth as silk,' he observed. 'No hidden impurities.' He rolled on to his back, pulling her on top of him and holding her face close while he kissed her lingeringly on the lips. 'No more British reticence either,' he added against the corner of her mouth. 'I told you I'd cure you of that!'

Eve laughed, moving with delicate deliberation against him. 'So you did. Shall I show you how far the cure goes?'

The dark brows were drawn together in a grimace, his teeth clenched. 'You were right the first time,' he ground out. 'We'd better get dressed.'

'I thought you said there was plenty of time,' Eve murmured.

'I lied. In roughly ten minutes from now Skip Williams is going to walk through those doors to finish loading bales.' It was Brett's turn to laugh as he watched her push herself hastily upright. 'Thought that might cramp your style! Maybe I should have kept my mouth shut and just let you get on with it.'

The thought of what this Skip might have stumbled on if he had let things carry on was past contemplation. Shorn of the all-consuming emotion of previous moments, her whole mood was undergoing a swift and depressing alteration. She and Brett were friends again—if that was the word for it—but nothing else had changed.

'Where do we go from here?' she made herself ask as she pulled on her clothing.

He sat up himself, reaching for the nearest garment. 'Let's just play it the way it comes.'

Eve glanced at him swiftly, hating him a little for not being all she would have wanted. Yet she had known from the first that tender speeches were not his style. 'You mean I should sit back and wait for you to contact me when you feel like it?'

'You know damned well that's not what I meant.' He stood up to tuck his shirt into his waistband, looking down at her with a faint twist to his lips. 'There's a lot needs straightening out before we can start thinking about any kind of future.'

'Like the Circle Three?' Her voice was very soft. 'You'd like me to give in over that, wouldn't you, Brett?'

'Yes, I'd like it.' There was no hesitation in the

reply. 'With you over there and me over here we're going to have problems to start with.'

She swallowed thickly. 'And if I agreed to sell out to you?'

'Then we could start afresh.'

'Except that I'd have lost my main attraction.'

He stopped what he was doing, eyes hardening. 'If you believe that there isn't a lot left to say.'

'I don't.' Her head was bent, fingers fumbling with the buttons of her shirt. 'Not really.'

'Not good enough.' A hand fastened under her arm, drawing her bodily to her feet and round to face him. He looked angry. 'You think I'm capable of faking the kind of response you've been getting—you think any man is?'

'No,' she said. 'Of course not.'

'Then stop talking like an idiot!' He studied her upturned face, his own suddenly relaxing. 'You underrate yourself, Eve.'

'So you said before.' She shrugged, trying to pass the moment off lightly. 'Better than the other extreme.'

'Is it? I'm not so sure.' Brett let go of her to finish fastening the buckle of his belt, running a hand through his hair before replacing his hat. 'Let's get out of here.'

It was only when he stopped to lift a saddle down from its hook on the wall that she remembered the reason they were here in the barn at all. Brett caught her eye as he shoved open the door with his shoulder, brows lifting quizzically.

'That's one subject we finished arguing the toss about, I hope?'

Eve followed him into the sunlight, blinking a little after the dimness inside. 'What's going to happen to the mare?' she asked.

'Nothing drastic. If it makes you happy I'll give her the run of the west pasture.' He hitched the saddle across one arm in order to swing open the gate to the corral. 'Come and meet your new mount.'

He had got his own way again, yet she could hardly fault his reasoning. Concern for her safety was at least a step in the direction she so desperately wanted his emotions to take.

CHAPTER TEN

SATURDAY was muggy and oppressive, with thunder rumbling in the distance but no rain to mar the occasion. Wade drove them across to the Diamond Bar, prevailed upon despite his professed reservations by Fleur's insistence that he squire the two of them.

'We don't know anybody apart from Brett and his father,' she pointed out, 'and they're likely to be too busy playing host.' Her smile would have weakened the firmest resolve. 'Anyway, *I* want you to come.'

It was her sister's emotions Eve was thinking about during the drive. Listening to the other two laughing and talking together in the front of the car, she wondered how much longer it could last. Even one short week was a long time by Fleur's standards. Normally by this time the initial impact would have faded, the new become commonplace and boring. One thing was certain, when she lost interest she would do it overnight. In the meantime there was little one could do but sit back and wait for it to happen.

Her own situation also remained static. Brett had made no attempt to get in touch over the past couple of days. Yet what could he have said? she reasoned, looking for comfort. He had known he would be seeing her again today. Along with a few dozen others, added a small insistent voice at the back of her mind. It was hardly the same thing.

The barbecue fires had been lit at the rear of the

house, with a couple of the ranch hands presiding. Long tables held a variety of accompaniments to the steaks and burgers and jacket potatoes already wafting deliciously mouthwatering aromas across the gathered throngs of people. Clad in close-fitting grey pants tucked into tooled leather boots, Brett was standing with a small group close by the house. A black kerchief fluttered lazily at the open neck of his tailored shirt. He saw them at the same moment they saw him, lifting a beckoning hand to bring the three of them over to his party. Wade received a scant nod of recognition.

There was no waiting for formal introduction, Eve discovered over the following moments. People identified themselves casually by name, often adding a helpful rider regarding their home location. Once having seen the two sisters launched, Brett moved off to greet another group of guests, swinging a buxom matron into a bear-hug to the accompaniment of ribald cheers from the rest of what appeared to be her large family. Eve tried to concentrate on her more immediate surroundings, but found it difficult. Her ears were tuned to the sound of Brett's laughter, the timbre of his voice. There would be no opportunity to be alone with him, that was fast becoming obvious. As host, he was in great demand.

Bart was enjoying himself hugely, swinging the wheelchair about as if it weighed nothing.

'Can't think why it's taken me so long to get round to doing this again,' he admitted to Eve as she bent to kiss his cheek. 'Anyway, it's been too long. What happened to that sister of yours?'

'See that circle of men over there?' Eve responded dryly, indicating the direction. 'The flash of pink in the middle—that's Fleur.'

Bart chuckled. 'Need I have asked! Your foreman doesn't look too chipper about it.'

Wade, Eve conceded, looked anything but. He stood on the fringe of the competition, thumbs hooked through the loops of his belt and an unconcealed scowl on his face. Any moment now, she judged, he was going to do one of two things: either he would simply walk away from the fray, or he would go in there and lay his own claim to the centre of it. Eve hoped it would be the former, if only for the reason that it might teach Fleur a lesson. She was exerting every ounce of her considerable charm in order to make Wade jealous—as she had done with others so many times before. It was time someone turned the tables on her. With his looks, Wade couldn't possibly find it difficult to do that.

'He'll cope,' she said. 'I'm ravenous! When do we eat?'

'Food's up!' somebody yelled above the general clamour, and Bart grinned.

'There's your answer. I could eat a horse myself! Want to try for second place?'

The line-up was already forming. Eve tagged on to the end of it with Bart at her back in the chair. The man at his rear started a conversation which claimed his whole attention. Standing with hands tucked idly into the deep pockets of her blue cotton skirt, Eve watched the other end of the line moving slowly along the serving counter and wondered where Brett had got to. If he was deliberately avoiding her he was making a good job of it.

The girl in front of her turned her head to wave to someone farther back in line, catching Eve's eye in sudden recognition.

'Hi!' she said. 'Remember me? I work at the diner in town.'

Eve nodded, smiling back. 'Sue-Ann, isn't it?'

'Hey, that's real good!' The pleasure was mixed with something else. 'I can never remember names.' There was a momentary hesitation and a subtle change of expression before she added a mite too casually, 'Somebody said you brought Wade Connors with you. Haven't seen him in ages.'

'I expect he's been busy,' Eve replied, too well aware where the girl's interest lay. 'Round-up, and all that.'

'Round-up was over more than a week ago,' came the flat response. 'I guess he's been busy with other things. Your sister's real pretty, isn't she.'

It was a purely rhetorical question, not really requiring any answer. Eve studied the undoubtedly pretty face in front of her and knew a pang of heartfelt sympathy. 'They barely know each other,' she said.

The girl's laugh had a bitter ring. 'No fault of Wade's! He told somebody we both know he wasn't going to let anybody else knuckle in on what he had going. You want to watch out for that sister of yours. Wade's not the only one who's going to be thinking about all that money your aunt left.'

Jealousy, Eve told herself quickly. Just plain, green-eyed jealousy. 'Fleur is more than capable of seeing through people,' she said, wishing suddenly that she could feel more convinced of it. 'And I don't think you should go around repeating things you've only heard from someone else. Words get twisted.'

'You'll see,' came the rejoinder. 'Wade Connors doesn't give up easy.'

Eve's eyes were drawn involuntarily back to the spot where she had last seen the Circle Three foreman, but there was no sign either of him or of Fleur. Sue-Ann had turned away, visibly affronted by the lack of acceptance on Eve's part. Jealousy might come into it, but there had been the ring of truth in what she had said. Eve touched her on the shoulder, summoning a brief smile as the blonde head jerked round again.

'Thanks,' she said softly.

The smile was returned, if with reluctance. 'It isn't fair, that's all. It was me he was interested in before he heard about you two. Mrs Cranley let him think he just about owned the whole ranch. He'd do anything to keep it that way. If he hadn't fancied your sister more he'd have tried for you.'

'He'd have been unlucky.' Eve was too incensed at her own lack of insight to keep a guard on her tongue. 'He isn't my type.'

'I know.' There was a certain blandness in the girl's regard. 'At least you'll never have to wonder if Brett Hanson is only after your money!'

Eve could feel the heat rushing up under her skin, and could do nothing to staunch it. 'I don't . . .' she began.

'I saw him take off after you on Wednesday. So did a lot of other folk.' Sue-Ann was enjoying the moment. 'You can't keep much secret round here. Anyway, you've been riding that Palomino of his this last couple of days. Everybody knows what that horse is worth—won every prize going this last three years.'

She left it there, reaching for a plate as the line moved up. Behind her, Eve did the same, her actions purely automatic. A prize animal! She should have known. Nothing so perfect could be anything else but. And why? There could be only one answer to that. The emotions welling inside her had nothing to do with gratitude.

There was still no sign of Fleur or Wade by the time she had finished eating. Hesitantly, not really liking what she was thinking, Eve made her way through the throng overflowing into the house itself, looking for the pair of them without success. She could hardly search the bedrooms too, she acknowledged ruefully. Not only was Fleur of an age to do as she chose, but she herself was in no position to cast any aspersions. All she could hope was that her sister would be prepared to heed the warning she was bound to pass on.

Brett came out from the study as she passed the door. 'I've been looking for you,' he said.

Eve gave him a straight, unsmiling glance. 'You were hardly likely to find me in there.'

He stepped in front of her as she made to walk on, eyes narrowed. 'Something biting you?'

'How about a prize-winning Palomino?' she demanded bitterly. 'What was he—payment for services rendered!'

The strong mouth snapped to a thin taut line. Without speaking Brett gripped her arm and shoved her past him into the room he had just vacated, closing the door behind him and leaning against it.

'Now say that again,' he invited.

She rubbed the spot where his fingers had dug into the soft flesh, the hurt still too raw to allow room for doubt. 'Isn't that what it amounts to? Perhaps I should be flattered. One thing you're not is tight-fisted!'

'One thing I might start to be is good and

rough!' he gritted. 'What the hell brought that little lot on?'

'You know what brought it on.' There was no way she was backing down now. Eyes stormy, she stood her ground, daring him to touch her. 'You can take him back—win some more prizes! Just give me my own property.'

'You cross-grained little fool!' He was furious, and unnerving with it, body tensed as if he were fighting the urge to do something drastic to her. 'Don't you ever stop to do any reasoning before you blow up?'

'About what?' she demanded. She was trembling a little, but with anger of her own, not apprehension. 'You knew what was going to happen the other afternoon. You arranged it so we'd be undisturbed just long enough for you to get *your* satisfaction!'

The laugh was anything but humorous. 'You're trying to tell me it was all one-sided?'

'No, I'm not.' The tremor was eradicated by sheer force of will. 'Which means you didn't need to bribe me with the gelding. I'd have supplied the same performance for nothing.' Head up, she moved forward. 'Now get out of my way!'

'Like hell I will!' He came away from the door in one savage movement, following her as some instinct of self-preservation backed her steps. 'You think I'm polecat enough to use what's available, so let's take it from there!'

The desk came up hard at the base of her spine, effectively stopping her in her tracks, but it didn't stop Brett. His weight bent her backwards across the cleared surface, pressing her down on to the unyielding wood until she thought her spine would snap. She opened her mouth to cry out, only to have it stopped by his. He was giving her no quarter. For the first time she felt fear enter her heart.

'Brett, no!' she gasped desperately the moment he eased the pressure to take a breath.

'Brett, yes!' he mimicked, grinding himself into her. The blue eyes were relentless. 'You asked for it, you're going to get it. You might even enjoy it!'

'You're breaking my *back*!' She choked the words between gritted teeth, almost passing out with the pain. 'Please . . .'

It was her pallor that got through to him. Suddenly the crushing weight was gone and he was lifting her upright, swinging her into his arms to carry her over to a sofa and lay her down on the cushions. Kneeling at her side, he looked into her face with eyes still brimming with anger, but with something else there too. Ruefulness? Regret? She wasn't sure.

'For God's sake stop doing this to me,' he muttered harshly. 'You're driving me round the twist!'

'I'm sorry.' Her voice was low, the lump in her throat too hard to swallow. 'It's no joke knowing what people are thinking about the two of us.'

'It doesn't matter what anyone else thinks,' he said. 'Or it shouldn't. It's between you and me, Eve. *Just* you and me. We'll sort something out.'

'What?'

He sighed, one hand coming out to smooth the line of her cheek. 'God only knows. You won't give up the Circle Three for me, will you?'

Her hesitation was brief enough to be almost non-existent. 'No.'

'Then we're in a cleft stick.' He ran a finger tip slowly down her throat to the base of the V formed by her sleeveless blouse, his jaw firming anew. 'There's only one way we're in accord, so let's make the most of it.'

Eve lay still as he slipped the three tiny buttons and pushed aside the flimsy material, needing his touch more than she needed her pride. Her breast swelled eagerly into his hand, the rose-tipped peak begging for his lips.

The crisp dark hair was thick and springy beneath her fingers. She tightened her grasp as his tongue flickered a long, slow passage across the valley between her breasts, breath coming harder and faster in rhythm with his own. His hand felt warm on her thigh, drawing response with its slow and subtle caress. There was a momentary pause while he readied himself, then he was over her and with her, and nothing else mattered a damn.

It didn't stay that way, of course. Memory eventually caught up. Cradling the dark head on her shoulder, Eve wondered what would really happen should she withdraw her opposition to the sale of the Circle Three. If Brett was only playing her along to that end then he had missed his true vocation, because there had never been a more convincing performance. What she lacked was the courage and self-confidence to put those same emotions to the test.

'We still didn't straighten things out about the Palomino,' she said softly, unable to bear her thoughts any more. 'He's too valuable to give away as a riding hack, Brett. If you still feel strongly about the mare, find me something else.'

The sigh came deep, though beyond turning his head slightly towards her he made no attempt to change his position. 'Whoever filled you in on the Palomino's background doesn't know too much about the show ring. Misty is a seven-year-old. He's taken major prizes the last three years, and that's long enough. If some idiot who didn't know what he was doing hadn't gelded him he'd have been put to stud. Failing that, the next best thing is a loving companion. He's too young and fit to be turned out to grass with the older animals. Giving him to you was the perfect solution.' The pause was brief but meaningful. 'Satisfied?'

'Yes.' This time the sigh was her own. 'You're right, I do jump to conclusions.'

'If that's an apology it's accepted.' He lifted his head enough to kiss her lightly on the mouth, then hoisted himself upright with a hand on the sofa back. 'Honey, we have to go. There are folk out there I'm supposed to be hosting.' The blue eyes started another slow burn as he looked down into her upturned face, at the spread of shining hair across the cushion. 'Duty's a hell of a thing at times. Meet me down by the bridge tomorrow afternoon, and we'll take a ride.'

'With or without the horses?' she asked, and could have bitten out her tongue as she saw his features tauten. 'I didn't mean that,' she added quickly.

'You meant it.' He got to his feet, adjusting his clothing without haste. 'Like I said, we're in a cleft stick. You're the only one with a way out. If it's assurances you want first, you're not going to get them.'

The elation had flown. Eve sat up, smoothing her skirt over her knees with hands that felt nerveless. 'Every time I have a bone to pick with you we finish up like this,' she said, attempting a lighter note. 'There has to be a moral in that somewhere.'

Brett's smile held little humour. 'There's nothing deep about it. We're two people who enjoy making love. A little provocation simply adds to it.'

Hazel eyes flashed. 'Why bother with euphemisms?'

'Because the basic term doesn't cover it in our case—at least, I didn't think it did.' He moved suddenly and forcibly, reaching down to draw her to her feet and hold her there in front of him with hands hard on her shoulders. 'I'm not giving up over the Circle Three, Eve. It's too important to me. If it's as important to you then that's it. We'll call it a day.'

She gazed at him for what seemed an age, desperately trying to read the mind behind the vivid blue eyes. When she moved it was almost against her will, her cheek going down to his chest. All right,' she whispered. 'I'll talk it over with Fleur.'

It was a moment before he reacted. The hand coming up to smooth her hair was soft in its touch. 'You won't regret it,' he said. 'Once that's out of the way we have a clear road.'

He still wasn't making any promises, Eve acknowledged painfully, but would she have wanted them anyway? An offer of marriage in exchange for land hardly suggestd the depth of emotion she needed him to feel. It was going to be up to her to make sure that feeling developed, and if the only way to Brett's heart was via his senses then that was the way she was going to go.

It was only when they were outside again that she remembered her original reason for going in. Wade was not in evidence, but the sight of Fleur surrounded once more by eager swains was reassuring. Her one concern now was the latter's likely response to an about-face on the subject of selling out the ranch. If her interest in Wade was of a more permanent nature than usual, then she herself might no longer be willing.

The sultriness of the atmosphere had not improved. It lay like a pall, creating a lethargy most of the revellers seemed determined to ignore. Darkness brought additional entertainment for the gathering in the shape of a group of musicians up from Sebring. Lamps were lit, and a space cleared for dancing. Eve went to sit alongside Bart, delighted to see the sparkle in his eyes as he watched the proceedings.

'It's like old times,' he said. 'I've seen folk I haven't seen in years—mostly because I've discouraged visitors. Brett's mother used to love these affairs.'

'Is Brett like her at all?' asked Eve.

'In some ways. Very strong-willed woman when it came to something that mattered to her. Knew when to give in, though. Not many like that.'

It was Eve's turn to smile, albeit with reluctance. 'Am I being got at?'

'Could be.' He glanced at her, his brows drawing together. 'You and Brett had another fight?'

'Nothing special.' She was watching the dancers, refusing to look at him. 'We've known each other less than two weeks. It isn't long.'

Bart grunted. 'Depends on the folk concerned. Only thing I know is I never saw that son of mine more riled up over anything or anybody.'

'Anger isn't the kind of emotion I'm looking for,' she murmured.

'It's a positive one. You two struck sparks off one another the minute you got together.'

'And two positives make a negative.'

'Stop being so damned snappy with the answers,' growled the rancher. 'Nothing puts a guy's back up quicker than a Smart Aleck female! I just said Brett's mother knew when to give in. She knew when to keep her mouth shut into the bargain.'

This time Eve had to turn her head, her lip caught between her teeth. 'I asked for that,' she admitted. 'I suppose it's a kind of defence mechanism.'

'You don't need it.'

It was time to change the subject. She did it as smoothly as she could. 'Talking of Smart Alecks, my favourite one didn't make it after all.'

'He had to go see a client. With lawyers it's . . .' He broke off, eyes fixed on the woman in white threading her way towards the two of them through the intervening crowd, his whole posture stiffening. 'Hell!'

The newcomer came to a halt immediately in front of the wheelchair, the man at her back staying there as if in protection from a rear attack. Eve didn't need to study the honey-blonde hair and palely perfect features to know who she was. She had a vivid mental picture of a couple rolling together on the grass as the one tried to escape the other. By Brett's own admittance, Diane had been doing the struggling, yet this woman in front of her hardly looked the type to allow herself to be put into any position not of her own choosing in the first place. Cool and composed, her voice exactly suited her appearance.

'Hallo, Bart,' she said. 'If we're going to settle out of court, I thought it might just as well be here.'

Bart had recovered swiftly from the initial shock. His regard was admirably unemotional. 'In the hope of upping the ante?' he demanded.

Diane smiled and shrugged. 'In the hope of making you understand I'm not prepared to take any less than the asking figure, at any rate. It's a simple choice, darling. I need the money.'

There was no one else close enough to overhear the conversation, although to judge from the glances cast their way, plenty of people had recognised the second Mrs Hanson. Eve made a half-hearted attempt to rise, only to feel Bart's hand on her arm, pressing her down again into her seat.

'You *need* two million?' he asked with irony.

The shrug came again. 'I have a lot of commitments.'

'Is this one of them?' nodding his head in the direction of the man at her rear.

The latter moved a step to bring him to Diane's side. He was the younger of the two by several fairly apparent years, his Italianate looks enhanced by the superbly cut white suit and dark silk shirt. Even his accent was designed to entrance the average female ear. 'I am Mrs Hanson's legal representative,' he announced smoothly. 'She is not here to be catechised!'

'Then she should have stayed away,' said Brett harshly, joining their little group from out of nowhere. 'There's nothing to stop you leaving right now.'

'Ah, Brett!' Diane's expression had undergone a faint and indecipherable change. 'Now is that any way for an hospitable Southerner to talk? We had a long journey, honey. Naturally, if I'd known there was a party tonight I'd have waited till tomorrow.

'You're welcome to stay over till then,' put in Bart, cutting across his son's reply. 'Give us time to talk in the morning before you leave.'

'Come to an arrangement, you mean? Michael has all the papers ready for signing.' Diane watched her husband's face as she added softly, 'I'm capable of taking it into court, Bart, and you wouldn't like that, would you? Imagine the detail they'd want. All the ...'

Eve got shakily to her feet. 'I think I should go,' she said.

'Oh, you must be Laura Cranley's niece,' exclaimed Diane, switching her attention. 'I heard about that. Lucky girl! There's a sister too, isn't there?'

'Yes.' Eve couldn't bring herself to glance in Brett's direction. 'I'm going to look for her.'

Leaving the four of them was one of the hardest things she had ever done, but it was a family affair and she wasn't family. Remembering the look in Brett's eyes when he had come on the scene just now, she doubted if she ever would be. Whatever Diane had once meant to him, he wasn't over it yet. The scars were still visible.

CHAPTER ELEVEN

LOOKING for Fleur had been an excuse, of course. In the end it was Fleur who found her in a corner of the verandah.

'I thought you'd decided on an early night or something,' she remarked, curling into a seat at her sister's side on the cane sofa. 'I hear the delectable Diane turned up, though nobody seems to know why. Do you know what's happening?'

'Not exactly,' Eve returned with truth. 'And what I do know is none of my business.'

'Pardon my curiosity.' Fleur stayed silent for a moment, her mood difficult to assess. When she spoke again her tone was over-bright. 'It's a fab party, don't you think?'

'Fab.' Eve didn't bother concealing the irony. 'Where did our stalwart foreman disappear to?'

The blonde head jerked as if pulled by an invisible wire. 'Home to pack his gear,' she said. 'I gave him three months' pay in lieu of notice. I hope that's okay with you?'

Eve stared at her, unable to comprehend what she was hearing. 'You fired him?' she got out at last. 'But . . .'

'But nothing. He asked for it.' Fleur's voice had risen. 'I was on to him from the word go—especially after he started blackening Brett's name—only I enjoyed stringing him along. The idiot didn't even have the sense to play it cool. He really thought I was so bowled over by his good looks I'd marry him at the drop of a hat!' Her laugh grated. 'As if I wouldn't have realised the money had to have something to do with it! What kind of a fool did he think I was!'

'What did he do?' Eve asked the question very quietly, feeling the wounded pride, the tearing hurt. 'Fleur, don't take *me* for an idiot.'

The collapse was sudden and complete, the tears glinting in her eyes. 'He tried to get me into bed with him this afternoon,' she choked. 'In someone else's house too! He was so convinced he had me exactly where he wanted me he couldn't even be bothered to keep up the pretence. He said you wouldn't like it if we got married so quickly because you were jealous of me, so we'd go away together and make you pay me half of what the ranch is worth. He had it all planned, right down to the last detail.' She knuckled her eyes like a child, only succeeding in smudging the mascara on her long lashes. 'How could he, Eve? He's only known me a week!'

'But he's known about us a lot longer than that.' Eve made no attempt to touch her sister, aware that physical sympathy of that nature was the last thing needed just now. 'To quote an ex-girl-friend of his, if he hadn't fancied you more he'd have made the same play for me. Wade Connors is what we'd have called a "sooner" back home. He has an eye open for opportunity. It's a good thing you weren't really in love with him.'

Fleur kept her head bent. 'I thought I was.'

'No, you didn't.' The tone was gentle but firm. 'In fact, you were already getting bored with him. You showed that this afternoon. Makes him even more of a fool if he couldn't see it for himself.' She paused. 'Unless he did see it and panicked. That would explain a lot.'

'Yes, well, I suppose you could be right.'
Already Fleur's recovery was under way, the liquid
brown eyes regaining some of their normal
vivacity. 'He really did think a bit too much of
himself!' She giggled suddenly. 'You should have
seen his face when I wrote out that cheque! He
couldn't believe it. I bet nobody ever did anything
like that to him before!'

Eve said dryly, 'It's doubtful if many would. He
doesn't deserve three months' pay, but I'm glad
you gave it to him. This way he can hardly come
back and complain he was treated unfairly.'

Fleur's face clouded again. 'Only problem is
finding another foreman to take over.'

Less than a couple of hours ago there would
have been no problem, acknowledged Eve with
hollow recollection. Right now, with Diane
Hanson still here on the premises, she couldn't
even bring herself to think about the future.

The brilliant flash of lace-like lightning preceded
a downpour of such startling suddenness it was as
if someone had turned on a gigantic tap in the sky.
People raced for cover, crowding on to the
verandah to wring out drenched clothing with a lot
of laughter and little concern.

'Been expecting it all day,' somebody said.
'There's a tornado warning out along the west
coast. Maybe it veered inland.' The man speaking
caught Fleur's widened eyes and chuckled, shaking his head. 'Now, don't you go worrying
none about that. We get twisters every year
round this time, but nobody ever got killed in
these parts.'

'Some comfort,' muttered Fleur as he turned
away to go indoors. 'Perhaps we should stay the
night, Eve? Nobody would mind.'

Eve rose abruptly to her feet. 'You stay if you want. I'd rather go home.'

'I let Wade take the car,' Fleur admitted with some reluctance. She flushed as her sister looked at her. 'Well, he had to have some kind of transport to go and pick up his things. I thought Brett would take us back.'

Brett was the last person Eve wanted to ask. There had to be others, however, who would be going in their direction. 'I'll go and see,' she said. 'Stay put, will you? I don't want to be searching for you when I do find us a lift.'

The house was thronged with bodies, some of them wearing towels instead of blouses or shirts, few of them showing any signs of leaving. Judging from the number of refilled glasses around, the party semed to have gained new life. Eve spotted Diane and her lawyer friend talking together in a far corner, but neither Bart nor Brett were in evidence.

She found Bart eventually in the study, closing her mind to the memory of her previous visit to the same room so little time ago. Her heart went out to his tired, defeated expression.

'I need to borrow a car,' she said. 'It's a long story, but Wade Connors took off in ours.'

Bart shook his head. 'I was coming to find the two of you. There's a storm warning out. Most folk are staying over till it clears.'

'Is that likely to be long?'

'Depends which way it heads. Right now we're feeling a corner of it. If it keeps on the same track we'll miss the worst.'

'I'd still rather head for home.'

His smile was grim. 'What you really mean is you'd rather be out of the way while that wife of mine is here. You're not on your own.'

There was no point in trying to deny it. Eve said softly, "Have you come to any decision yet?"

'About the settlement?' His shoulders lifted. 'I don't have much choice.'

'You could fight it.'

'Did you ever sit in on a divorce case?' he asked dryly. 'They leave no stone unturned. I'd as soon pay the two million as have my private and personal affairs made public that way.'

'But it's so unfair!' Eve burst out. 'What did she ever do for you to merit that amount of money?'

The shrug came again. 'She gave me a whole year. I can't say it was a bad one. Could be she'd have stayed if I hadn't taken that toss. Then again, could be she wouldn't.' His gaze was steady. 'She wasn't in love with me, but we got along okay. Maybe I owe her something for that.'

'Not two million dollars!'

'You sound like Brett. He'd have me cut her off without a penny if I could get away with it. Extremists, the pair of them!'

Don't bracket them together! Eve wanted to shout. It took everything she had to stop the inner conflict from showing in her face. 'I'm sorry,' she said. 'I shouldn't even be making comments.'

'Why not?' His tone was gruff. 'You're as near family as I could ever want.' He studied her, his mouth slanting. 'You could be even closer if you'd come down off that stand you've taken.'

The words were jerked from her. 'I might have done, once.'

'Before you saw the way Diane looked at him tonight?'

Eve straightened away from the chair back where she had been leaning, face closing up. 'I don't . . .'

'It's okay—I always knew she fancied him—more so when she realised he didn't care for her. A woman her type likes a challenge.'

So why fight when success was within her grasp? Eve wondered numbly. Bart had it wrong. Brett was the real culprit. No matter how deeply he had coveted his father's wife, there was no excuse for what he had done.

'It *was* one-sided,' Bart insisted, watching her. 'There was talk—there always would be in our kind of community—but it was just talk. I know my own son, Eve.'

Her smile felt stiff. 'I'm sure you do. I'd better go and tell Fleur we're staying. Would you think it very rude of me if I went to bed? My head's splitting!'

'Probably the pressure,' he returned, making her feel a fraud because the sympathy was genuine and the headache only partially so. 'Best way is to sleep it off.' He shifted his chair back from the desk. 'I guess I'll rejoin the masses again myself before that wife of mine comes looking for me. Can't leave it all to Brett.'

Brett's present whereabouts was a question Eve refrained from asking. She had no desire to see him. Not until she had her emotions well in hand.

The wind had risen during the last fifteen minutes, driving everyone in off the verandah. Big as the living area was, it was filled to overflowing with people large and small. Fleur was deep in animated conversation with a couple of the younger male element, responding to the news of their cancelled departure with a smile and a wave of her hand without bothering to turn her pretty head.

A glimpse of a white suit on the far side of the

room indicated Diane's position. Of Brett there was still no sign. Eve assumed they were to use the rooms they had used before, although she was more than willing to share with Fleur if others also needed accommodation. The door stood slightly open. With her hand already on the knob, she froze into immobility as the voice reached her ears, mocking, taunting, wholly vindictive:

'You never could bear to think of me with your father, could you, darling? He was a whole lot of man before his accident—more than you might guess. I don't mind who knows what our intimate life was like, but he would—especially if I told them how he liked roughing me up.' The laugh jarred. 'They'd believe it. I have a vivid imagination, and a great way with words. I might even tell them about his son too. Share and share alike was his motto!'

'Bitch!' The word came low and biting, drawing another of the jangling laughs.

'Hitting me wouldn't do you any good, sweetie. Bruises show up well on photographs. You brought me in here to make me a proposition, so why not get on with it? I'll consider anything so long as it comes to two million minimum.'

Eve stayed to hear no more. Trembling, scarcely knowing where she was going or what she intended doing, she somehow made her way out to the verandah, clutching at a post as the wind tore at her skirt. The rain had stopped for the moment, although the sky was black as pitch except for the frequent flicker of lightning to the west. One of the ranch jeeps was parked close by the step. The keys would be in the ignition; nobody out here ever bothered to remove them. Without stopping to think about it, Eve went down and got behind the wheel. If it started to rain again she got wet, that was all. Anything rather than stay here in this house with that woman in residence!

Hair whipping about her face, she started out for the homestead gates, driving slowly in order to dodge any scattered debris. The headlights seemed to be working on half power, their glow reflected back by the darkness of the landscape. A television aerial came clattering down from one of the mobile homes as she passed the end of the row, banging against the slatted sideboards. Eve put her foot down a little on reaching the open road. Something nasty was building; she could sense it in the air. The sooner she was safely indoors again the better.

It took her a good twenty minutes to cover the few miles to the Circle Three. The car in which they had travelled out to the Diamond Bar was parked outside the foreman's quarters, the front end slewed as if it had been brought to a sudden and violent halt. There were no lights burning in the cabin, nor any sign of the blue station wagon belonging to the former occupant. Furious though he must have been at his summary dismissal, Wade Connors had left the ranch. Eve was too weary and dispirited to consider where that left them. Tomorrow would be time enough to start thinking ahead.

She was opening the house door when the noise struck her ears, faint and faraway at first but growing louder by the second—like a roaring freight train coming across open country. Dark though it was, the towering funnel of the tornado stood out clearly against the skyline, its lower end tapering to a slender point. It was coming this way, that much she ascertained in the one brief, terrifying glance.

Her only refuge lay inside. Even as the thought came to her she was moving, slamming the door to behind her and sliding the bolt in an instinctive though futile attempt to hold the twister at bay. It was that same instinct of self-preservation which drove her towards the kitchen and the basement door. Down there she would be partially below ground. It had to afford some protection.

As in most American homes, the basement area ran the full length and breadth of the building, divided into compartments by plasterboard walls. At some time in the past, Jos Cranley had turned one such space into a viewing room for home movies, with seating ranged along the length of one wall. Eve grabbed cushions and curled herself into a corner with as many as she could pile on top of her.

The unearthly noise shrieked in her ears, the pressure building until she thought the drums would burst. There was a moment when the house itself seemed to shift above her, then everything exploded into blackness.

She came round to darkness and the sound of dripping water, lying quite still for several dazed moments until her mind cleared. A large and heavy beam lay across her at hip level, the jagged lump of concrete on which it rested holding its crushing weight just barely touching her body. One false move could bring the whole lot down on her. Eve braced herself to stay as motionless as possible, wondering desperately how long she had been unconscious and whether anyone would have missed her yet. The latter seemed unlikely. So far as Bart was concerned, she had gone to bed. It might even be morning before her absence became obvious, and by then it could well be too late.

Looking upwards, she found she could see straight out through the gaping hole to a night sky torn by scudding cloud. Most of the house appeared to be gone. Eve felt hysterial laughter welling inside her. That solved one problem anyway!

At this moment and from this position none of her other concerns seemed worth a great deal. Oddly enough, considering her danger, she could even rationalise her emotions. If Brett was worth anything at all to her—and he was—then it didn't matter what he had done or been in the past. Now was all that counted. That, and any future they might have together. Might being the operative word, she thought, closing her eyes as the beam settled another half inch. If that concrete gave the weight would crush her spine, always providing it didn't kill her altogether. Of the two alternatives, she would prefer the latter. It had taken Bart three hard years to adjust to his disability; a lifetime wouldn't be long enough for her to do the same.

Subconsciously, she had almost accepted that the Circle Three employees domiciled here on the homestead must all be dead, or injured too badly to render her any assistance, so the sound of voices came as a shock that dried her throat. Her shout was a whisper, barely carrying beyond the confines of her immediate surroundings. She coughed as a cloud of concrete dust trickled down from above, freezing as the beam moved again. Oh, God, she thought, not now!

A flashlight probed the ruins not too far away from where she lay. Somehow Eve summoned the nerve to call out, terrified that even the slightest vibration would be enough to finish her. The voice that answered was familiar enough to bring tears of relief to her eyes. The hows or wherefores of his being here at all so soon were totally by the way. Brett would get her out, if anyone could.

His approach was cautious, one glance down the pit where she lay enough to assess the situation.

'I'll be right there,' he said. 'Just hold tight.'

Eve heard him giving instructions to others through a kind of fog as her mind registered the odds against survival. The way the beam was balanced, even the tying on of a rope to lift it could so easily tip the scales. Yet what was the alternative? Sooner or later the thing was going to go away. A slight chance was better than none at all.

He brought another man with him when he came, the two of them picking their way through the rubble of the basement from what was left of the stairway. Eve squeezed her eyes half closed as the flashlight swung her way, unable to see beyond the glare to the face of the man holding it.

'One more minute,' he said reassuringly. 'Ray, you get a hold on her and yank her out when I shout.'

'You'll never do it,' Eve breathed, guessing what he was about to attempt. 'Brett, it's too heavy for you!'

He ignored her, stepping carefully across to where the end of the beam rested so precariously, and kneeling to brace a shoulder beneath it. The cowpoke slid his hands very gently beneath Eve's armpits, tightening his grasp with a murmured encouragement.

'Okay,' said Brett. 'Now!'

It was over before Eve could draw breath, the great weight of wood crashing down on the very spot where she had lain bare seconds after her legs were clear. Then Brett was there with her, lifting her in his arms to press his face to her cheek in a manner which left nothing in doubt.

'Let's get out of here,' he said gruffly.

They were in the open air before Eve could bring herself to stop clinging to him so hard. He didn't put her down, but carried her across to the station wagon parked several yards from the ruined house and slid her into the front seat.

'I'm taking you home,' he said. His smile was wry. 'There's nothing left for you here.'

'Nothing I'd want,' Eve agreed softly. She put up both her hands and pulled him down to her, kissing him on the lips with a tenderness new to them both. 'I love you, Brett. You were there when I needed you. Nothing else matters but that.'

He touched her cheek, the expression in his eyes all she could have hoped for. 'We have a lot to talk about.'

There seemed to be people all over the place now, bringing a kind of order to the chaos left by the storm. Eve looked at her watch, then put it to her ear, amazed not only to find it still ticking merrily away but that it could still need another hour to midnight.

'We should stay and help,' she murmured as Brett came round to slide in beside her. 'How many were injured?'

'You, the house and one of the barns were the only casualties,' he said. 'Twisters are like that—selective.' He started the engine, turning his head to look at her with a smile. 'I've never been a fatalist, but there has to be some purpose behind what happened tonight. With both house and foreman gone, you can forget this commitment of yours about keeping the Circle Three going. Even Jos would have allowed that much.'

'Who told you about Wade?' she asked.

'Fleur did. She also mentioned the way you'd looked the last time she saw you.' The wry quality was there again. 'I put two and two together and came up with an obvious answer. You knew I'd been with Diane, didn't you?'

'I overheard a little of the conversation, yes,' she admitted.

'And jumped to a conclusion?'

She hesitated before answering. 'From what I did hear there was only one conclusion to draw. I'm not damning you for something that happened years ago. She's a very beautiful woman.'

'And you still believe I'm a sucker for looks.' His tone had hardened. 'Maybe I should let you go right on believing it.'

Eve sat still and silent as he put the car into motion, her heart heavy. It couldn't be going wrong again—not so soon. Why did they have to be at cross-purposes all the time? Was it her fault?

'You wanted to explain about that time Wade Connors saw you with Diana once, and I wouldn't let you,' she said at last. 'I'd listen now, Brett—and I'd believe.'

The strongly etched features remained in profile. 'I doubt it.'

'Try me,' she begged.

It was a moment or two before he responded, bringing the car to a stop at the roadside and sitting there with both hands on the wheel while he contemplated the darkness beyond the reach of his headlights.

'It isn't a pretty story,' he said. 'And I'm not faultless. I set out to prove something to myself. Whether I'd ever have have told Dad the truth is something I'll never really know. He took that fall a couple of days after Connors saw the two of us down by the river. The rest you know.'

Eve said carefully, 'I'm still not sure I understand. You admitted Diana was struggling to get away from you that time.'

'True enough. I'd just told her exactly what she was and why I'd made a play for her.' His mouth slanted. 'She didn't like it much.'

That had to be the understatement of the year. With recent experience in mind, Eve could well imagine the vitriolic reaction. There was no doubt left. Everything fitted so perfectly.

'I've been a fool,' she stated ruefully. 'I should have given you a chance.'

The shrug was brief. 'You didn't know me well enough to trust me. You still don't, if it comes to that.'

'I'm learning.' She put out a hand to his arm, sliding along the bench seat to rest her cheek against the smoothness of his shirt. 'I'm learning all the time. Hold me, Brett.'

He responded roughly, tipping up her face to a kiss that started with one kind of passion and finished with another. 'You haven't given me a minute's peace since the day I walked into that hotel lobby and saw you sitting there with that British bulldog look on your face,' he growled in her ear. 'You'd better start boning up on American marital relationships!'

Eve laughed, loving the feel of those long lean fingers at her breast; feeling the need and desire growing in him. 'From what I've seen of American wives so far I think I'm going to be right on form,' she said. 'You'd hate a docile mate!'

It was Brett's turn to laugh. 'Chance might be a fine thing!' There was a moment's pause as he looked at her, his mind concentrated by sheer sensation, then he smiled and took up her hand, kissing her fingertips with a tenderness that said so much. 'We're going home.'

He had the car moving again before she could find the right words. In the end there was only one way to ask the question. 'What about Diane?'

'She left,' came the calm reply. 'If you'd hung around a few minutes longer, you'd have seen her go. Her and that gigolo of hers.'

'Lawyer,' Eve corrected automatically. She glanced at him swiftly, trying to guess what was in his mind and failing as usual. 'So she won after all?'

'No, she didn't.' The blue eyes switched her way for a fleeting moment, expression amused. 'Just itching, aren't you?'

'Yes,' she admitted. 'Don't tease me, Brett. What really happened?'

'I faced her with a few plain facts,' he said. 'New to her, too, to give her some credit.'

'I don't understand . . .' Eve began, and heard him sigh.

'If you'll keep quiet long enough I'm trying to tell you. I did some checking this last couple of days. I knew she'd been married and divorced once already, only it never occurred to me to follow that angle before. Anyway, it seems she got a quickie at the time—maybe she had reason to be in a hurry. To get to the bottom line, it wasn't valid in this state.'

Realisation was swift and startling. 'You mean

she and your father were never really married at all!'

'That's about the size of it.' Brett was enjoying the effect of his disclosure. 'I could hardly believe it myself, but it's true enough. Doesn't leave her with a leg to stand on so far as the law is concerned. She could still find herself slapped with a bigamy suit. All Dad has to do is file for an annulment.'

Eve said worriedly, 'How are you going to tell him?'

'I already did.' The grin was pure pleasure. 'I haven't heard him laugh like that in years! I'd say it's given him a new lease of life.'

'What a relief!' Eve felt almost lightheaded with it herself. She looked misty-eyed at the man she was going to marry. 'You're terrific, do you know that?'

He smiled. 'Don't go overboard! I got across you before, I'll surely do it again.' There was a pause, and a subtle change of tone. 'How are you feeling?'

'Not up to what you have in mind,' she retorted promptly, and saw the smile come again.

'Am I that obvious?'

'Only sometimes.' She added on a softer note, 'And it isn't that I don't want you either, just that I'm covered in grit and grime and longing for a nice warm shower first.'

'We'll share it,' he declared. 'Like old times. Another three days and we'll have known one another two whole weeks! I guess I got myself well and truly hooked.'

'You surely did.' Eve let a moment or two of sheer happiness drift by before bringing her mind to bear on certain pressing matters. 'Brett, what's going to happen to the Circle Three hands? They all had jobs today, tomorrow they don't.'

The groan came from down deep. 'I wondered how long it was going to take!'

'If you knew the question was coming,' she said, 'you must have an answer ready.'

'Okay, so I already thought about it. Point number one, it isn't going to be an overnight dispersement. Auctions of stock and machinery take time to arrange. Between times, they all need keeping up to scratch. I can take on three, maybe four of your hands later on, complete with families where applicable, the rest I'll find jobs for elsewhere if needs be.' He paused, waiting. 'Anything else?'

'Just one thing.' Her tone was deceptively mild. 'You can pay Fleur half a million for her share of the land, the other half I'm giving to you as a wedding present.'

'That you're *not*!' The emphasis cracked like a gunshot. 'You can do what you like with the damned money, but I buy that land fair and square. Understood?'

There were moments, Eve reflected, when discretion was by far the better part of valour. This was definitely one of them. What was half a million, after all? She could always find a worthy cause.